The Geaha Incident

Patricia E. Canterbury

PEGASUS BOOKS

Pegasus Books
3338 San Marino Ave
San Jose, CA 95127
www.pegasusbooks.net

First Edition: September 2016

Published in North America by Pegasus Books. For information, please contact Pegasus Books c/o Christopher Moebs, 3338 San Marino Ave, San Jose, CA 95127.

This book is a work of fiction. Any resemblance to actual persons, living or dead, events, or locales is entirely coincidental.

Library of Congress Cataloguing-In-Publication Data
Patricia E. Canterbury
The Geaha Incident/Patricia E. Canterbury 1st ed
p. cm.
Library of Congress Control Number: 2016953170
ISBN – 978-1-941859-56-8

1. FICTION / Science Fiction / General. 2. FICTION / Mystery & Detective / Women Sleuths. 3. FICTION / African American / Mystery & Detective. 4. FICTION / Science Fiction / Space Opera. 5. PETS / Birds. 6. FICTION / Family Life.

10 9 8 7 6 5 4 3 2 1

Comments about *The Geaha Incident* and requests for additional copies, book club rates and author speaking appearances may be addressed to Patricia E. Canterbury or Pegasus Books c/o Christopher Moebs, 3338 San Marino Ave, San Jose, CA, 95127, or you can send your comments and requests via e-mail to cmoebs@pegasusbooks.net.

Also available as an eBook from Internet retailers and from Pegasus Books

Printed in the United States of America

Dedicated to

Dr. Richard Lipon

Sydney Velasquez Rasberry, my niece and inspiration for Jamaica

THE GEAHA
INCIDENT

Prologue

Peace has finally arrived on Earth. Murder is rare and found mostly among the wild men and women of the frontier on orphan moons or windy, frightening and dangerous planets on the edge of the Milky Way. Within our solar system, the last remaining haven for outlaws is the 23rd moon of Uranus. The law enforcement personnel who bring these rogue beings to justice are members of an Interplanetary Corps [Timossi], who are called tracers. Jamaica Wong is a second year tracer. It is 2310 and the middle of the twenty-five year reign, when the Earth acted as host of the Timossi's Headquarters.

The majority of deaths are from accidents or old age in a time when many live into their middle 100s. Most diseases have been eradicated. Those that remain originated from alien species attempting to adapt to Earth's atmosphere.

###

In the prior century, 2207, plant based materials became the source for all interactive devices such as computers, communication instruments and the new technology of halovision.

Chapter 1

"Danger... danger... danger."

The alarm light module awakened Kalt, captain of the Geahan space ship, *ZIXC*. Fully awake, she looked around as the alarm continued its bright, harsh purple emergency warnings. It bathed her hibernation pod in a brilliant purple light and rocked her violently around in the confined pod space. Holding on to the edge of the pod, she felt around for her weapon, a clear, deadly Geahan ice probe, which fit safely in her left hand, and exited slowly. She found herself staring into a black unfamiliar sky.

"Oh no, what is this?" she asked aloud, looking into an inky black sky with its brilliant stars and a large, cloudy, planet looming on the edge of the horizon.

Placing her translucent three-fingered left hand over her three small hearts, each finger resting on the hollow beatings, she tried to quiet her sense of alarm.

"Calm yourself, you need to think clearly." She continued her solitary visual inspection, checked and double-checked the ship's instruments. Her high-pitched musical voice echoed between beats of the "danger... danger..." still coming from the alarm.

"Strange, the instruments are working properly, but the ship is damaged." Looking out the visual screen as the ship continued the rocking motion that awakened her, she checked the gyro computer, and once again, consulted the star map.

She looked at the star map again and gasped.

"The Heru Cluster, which should be here, to my right, is

not in my vision path. We seem to be in the midst of a jumble of stars and planets so dense that the light had a 'leche' cast," Kalt continued her one-sided conversation with growing alarm and staggered down the stairs to the crews' chambers.

"Good, all are still in deep hibernation," she said, checking each hibernation pod. The pale green glow of their pods enveloped her crew, who were unaware of her distress.

"What will I tell them when they awaken?" she asked the star-crowded sky, as she continued to hold onto solid objects so that the ship's rocking motion did not send her crashing to the floor.

"There's plenty of food," Kalt said, checking the galley.

With the use of her light waves, she recorded onto the ship's log, which blinked and glowed with yellow, blue, green and purple instrumentation. Looking to the left of the galley, she stared in alarm at the passage of time recorded on the Geahan poes, their time pieces.

"This cannot be. We left our home planet, Geaha, just twelve solar months ago. We have been in hibernation since then. We should be nearing Heru's sun, Seiu, but we are not. I cannot find Heru anywhere." Kalt continued to check her instruments and look into the vastness of the unfamiliar sky.

Kalt's people, the Geahans, were an ancient race that had inhabited the planet, Geaha, and its sister planets for millions of centuries. The Geahans were transparent in solar light to all but other Geahans, and were humanoid, but they had three fingers and three hearts. Their outline could be seen by non-Geahans only in total darkness. Their sense of direction—left, right, up and down—had been adjusted to earth's orientation for the past thousand years. They communicated in forms of color; they heard audio waves through sensors in their fingertips. Their empaths were reported to be excellent vocal linguists and physicians.

The Geahans perfected space travel about 6,000 years ago. All was quiet and peaceful for thousands of years. Wars with neighbors had been eliminated through negotiation. The Geahans worked to perfect art, medicine, education and sports.

Five years earlier, the crew of the research ship, *Layi*, had unwittingly brought a plague to the planet. The plague slowly infected the Geahans' central nervous system, making them unable to float in Geahan atmosphere. Grounded, the affected Geahans became disoriented and unable to speak in color. All their words became pale grey. Since the affected Geahans were unable to float, they had to be carried or drag themselves across the planet's surface. Breathing was extremely difficult, and those affected soon turned a dull orange as realization of their fate set in.

Babies and children under the age of ten were not yet affected. The elderly, some of whom lived for nearly 300 Geahan years, died within a week of infection. Kalt's ship, *ZIXC*, was bringing the planet a supply of serum, which was discovered accidentally when one of a group of infected explorers ate a small yellow bean found on a distant moon. It was believed this unnamed bean could eliminate the plague that had nearly destroyed the sentient life forms on the planet. But the ship had disappeared.

Though many thought space to be a vacuum, a strong solar wind current flowed between planets orbiting their main sun. The wind rivers were discovered in the late Twenty-first century. Most of the ships that sailed between planets were designed much like the ancient Earth schooners of the Sixteenth century. The ship's five-masted sails were made from spun gold, and although the texture of worn cotton they had the strength of titanium.

"I need to think. Too many thoughts are crowding my

mind. I need help. Where are we?" Kalt asked herself, while the unsteady ship still tossed her about. She reached the holding pod where her first officer, Plas, slept, and attempted to release the hibernation mist.

"Plas, wake up. We're in the middle of a fierce storm. The wind is very intense." The hibernation mist released on the second attempt and she slowly awakened him. "The ship is severely damaged, but the crew is well," she said, holding onto the solid hibernating/sleeping pod on which he lay. He reached for her hand, her three fingers—slender, strong, and iridescent—caught the light and changed colors as she spoke.

Wearing a frown, he concentrated on her words.

"You are not making any sense," he said, his deep bass/red voice echoed off the smooth ship walls. As he sat up, Plas became aware of the extent of the ship's damage.

"What happened?" he asked, as he floated onto spilled liquids and over broken objects. He joined Kalt as she pointed out damages, including splits, alterations and tears to the ship's inner body.

"Is the cargo intact?"

Nodding, Kalt continued to look around.

"How long before the crew is awakened?" Plas asked. "Is the damage life threatening?" he continued, preventing her answer to his first question. Caught in the light, his skin glowed deep blue, then purple. He bent his small head close to Kalt's mouth and placed his second finger on her mouth to calm some of her fears.

"The crew will awaken in a solar day. That is if my calculations are correct and we last that long. Do you have any idea where we are?" Her skin glowed blue, then purple, matching his in worry.

"You know the answer. But let me check. No, I do not know where we are. We do not appear to be within our own solar system," he answered, verifying her calculations.

"What is that? It looks like a large cloudy planet? There are no planets like that one in...." The ship's sudden uncontrolled downward spiral toward the planer interrupted his words.

"The navigational gauge has ceased functioning!" Kalt shouted above the harsh purple warning alarms.

"The increasing violent solar winds, clocked at over a million knots, buffeted ships sailing between Mbongo, the Martian artificial space station staffed by robots, and Vos, the Venusian space station with top secret military personnel staffing. All the sailing ports on the Vosian space station, the *Bole*, are full. The ports of the Earth station, the *Galileo*, are nearing capacity. The Naresh station—the station nearly on the far side of Venus and the one further from the others—the *Clea*, is nearly deserted. Only three Naresh ships are moored in a dock that can hold 360." The Vosian weather forecaster's mechanical sounding voice, speaking in a slow cadence above the daily hum of the three space stations did not mention the arrival of the *ZIXC* on the far side of Vos nor of the inhabitants' increasing distress. The space stations appeared to be a small full moon when viewed from each home base, yet it took nearly an earth week to travel from one to another. However, the *ZIXC* did not go unnoticed by the space station's ultra-secret solar array, which sent a coded message to the Tommosi headquarters on Earth.

The alarms aboard the *Bole* sounded milliseconds after the weather report. Collision alarms sounded simultaneously throughout the *Galileo* and the *Clea*. All the ships sailing toward the space stations abruptly stopped their forward movement as an invisible force field enveloped the ships, as if protecting them from harm. Confusion filled the various command stations.

The solar wind that continued to blow grew in strength as the *ZIXC* continued its spiral to the cloudy planet. The tumbling ship rendered Kalt and Plas unconscious and sent them crashing to the floor of the navigational station. Just before losing consciousness Kalt sent an SOS scout probe to her sister ships. The *ZIXC* sighed, burped, tore, folded within itself and for a brief moment collapsed. Then it re-expanded and drifted toward the *Clea,* on the far side of Vos.

"High Commissioner, Ncha, It is I, Adno, commander of the *Llbe.*"

"Yes, yes, Adno. Welcome, is there word of the *ZIXC?* Is the serum safe?"

"High Commissioner, there has been a time rip. We have been out of communication with our sister ships for a Mych. By the time communication was restored the *ZIXC* was gone. She is the only ship carrying our serum."

"Gone? Then we are doomed," Ncha said in a low voice, his skin glowing purple, then soft green. He resumed the seat he had left to acknowledge the ship's communication and looked into the information crystals, speaking so softly that those close to him did not hear.

"Call the leaders. We must determine when to tell the public of the *ZIXC's* loss... of our loss," His words glowed purple, filling his small thought chamber, then evaporated before those who stood around the thought table could capture them.

"High Commander, the people must not know of the *ZIXC's* fate until all hope is gone," said an elderly female empath, who also glowed purple. Her gossamer gown scattered dark blue sparks of anxiety into the atmosphere.

"The public could not take the news," another purple being said in a harsh tone, his pale yellow words cutting the Geahan next to him so deeply he bled.

"We must prepare an alternative," said another, more softly shaping the yellow words to a smoother green.

"The doctors must find a solution to the plague here, on Geaha," a young, green-glowing female said, in dismissal of the purple aria of her elders, putting a yellow caste back into the air.

"We have been meeting for weeks; waiting like *Noxa* for *ZIXC*," she continued with disgust—blue mixed with green—masking her worry.

"I do agree that the Geahan people should not learn of the *ZIXC's* disappearance until all hope is lost," Ncha said.

"The plague is now in its fourth year. It has killed one in every hundred Geahans. The serum was our last hope. We must pray that the ship and crew are safe and will return before it is too late." He continued to ease from his hard marble bench and flowed to the oval windows to gaze at the deep pink sky. He turned to face the leaders of his planet and absorbed their guilt; their blue, purple, and green thoughts gathered close and enveloped him.

"We must keep the color, just last night my only child, my fairest daughter died from the plague. As much as the masses, I also hope for the serum. We must conduct the *Sixth Sheep*."

"The *Sixth Sheep*? It is for children. Is that all you can recommend? What can we do if the *ZIXC* is truly lost? If the crew is dead and the serum lost? It would mean extinction for a whole species of beings. And you think of the *Sixth Sheep*." The young, green female counselor cried as she swiftly flowed from the council chamber.

Caught in the solar winds Kalt's probe headed toward the cloudy planet.

"What's that?" a young ensign fresh from military school and new to the *Clea* asked in a loud voice.

"What's what? I don't see anything. You're always seeing things," his good-natured station mate, a seasoned veteran of the *Clea*, teased as he looked in the direction the ensign pointed.

"There," the ensign answered, pointing in the direction of Vos. "I thought I saw a large purple flash."

"I still don't see anything. You're probably getting sun blindness from all this light here on the station."

"Wait, what is that?"

"It's a... it's a... it looks like a large bubble-like object, approaching us from the far side of Vos. It will be here soon."

"Why aren't the sensors reacting?" The men turned and started to speak but neither had time to register alarm. They were dead in seconds. Their families on the planet Tapia were too far away to feel the death dirge at once. The wailing began at Tapia's dawn, ten hours after their deaths.

The *ZIXC,* containing the unconscious and hibernating Geahans, continued in the direction of the *Clea.* The alarms persisted on the *Clea* for hours as visitors and residents scrambled for safety. The control room personnel scanned the sky; the wheat-based computers blinked, hummed and resumed the alarms.

"There is nothing out there that we can see," Jiangan officers said to their senior officers who relayed the information to commanders, who radioed to Tapia.

Deep within the *Clea's* air pumps, liquid methane—the Jiangans' life source—was beginning to crystallize. The doses, too small to register on the state-of-the-art dandelion-root computer terminals, went unnoticed.

The *Bole* and the *Galileo* went on alert. The heavens appeared clear, yet collision alarms on all three space stations sounded.

"Please identify yourself," anxious personnel asked ships when they approached the station.

"What's going on? Why are we being held on the far side of the Carpenter Barrier?" the equally anxious ships' captains asked.

"The collision alarms are sounding. We haven't identified the source of the distress. There may be a rogue ship approaching."

"Collision alarms? Rogue ships? There's nothing out here but us. Why would the alarms be sounding? It must be a malfunction of your equipment."

"The alarms are sounding on all the space stations."

"Then it must have something to do with the material of the station and not with my ship. Allow us to dock."

"We cannot. The *Clea* has reported the deaths of two young ensigns in their observation tower. Both bodies have turned to dust."

"Dust?"

The incredible shouts from a dozen ships' captains tumbled over each other.

"Yes, dust. Their uniforms appear unmarked. The *Clea's* medical personnel do not have enough residual body substance to determine cause of death."

"Enough! We do not wish this information shouted throughout the galaxy," a *Clea* Senior Commander said as he blocked the rest of the outgoing information.

"Doctors, tell me what has happened?" he asked, walking past the shaded observation station and past the small dust residues, which were all that was left of the ensigns.

"Sire, the young men were from Tapia. The older, O-113 has been on the *Clea* for a year; the younger, OO2-6, for only a month. Both are... were respected military personnel who volunteered for space station duty. Sire, they knew the danger. They knew that the intense light from the sun makes duty here... hazardous and extremely... profitable."

"Uh huh. Keep me informed. Why weren't these men in uniform?"

"Sir, they were in uniform. Complete to the netsuke fasteners as required while on duty. We cannot understand why their uniforms are now white. Or what happened to the men's bodies?" the visibly shaken Commanding Officer, 00-4-69 a grizzled old veteran of the Saari Wars, replied.

I don't like mysteries. I'm going to make this my personal agenda to get to the bottom of this trouble, he thought, glaring at his old enemy,

General 0-24-3, who turned on his heels and left Commanding Officer 00-4-69, staring at his back.

So the unspoken challenge had begun. Only one of us will be rewarded for solving the cause of the men's deaths, 00-4-69 thought, smiling in spite of the tragic deaths.

"I must send the dirge to their families," he said aloud, but there was no one in range to hear him. He turned and exited the empty observation chamber.

The chaos began immediately, regardless of the space stations' calming interior voice telling all inhabitants to remain calm; all is well; this is a training exercise; ignore the alarms. Humans and other beings reverted to survival instinct, cried, fought and looted things they could never use off the station. They stampeded and drank as each and every individual attempted to make sense of the nonsense surrounding them. Children asked questions without answers, teachers searched computer files, even ancient ones looked for clues, as to what was causing the constant alarm? Was the station going to explode? Had some unseen force already invaded the stations?

Many reverted to ancient fears as the space stations' bars quickly filled with the stunned personnel of various species who whispered among friends, avoided contact with superiors, looked confused and increasingly suspicious of strangers. Some thought they might be going mad, or that something far beyond their capability to understand was happening, and knew they were in the dark.

"McPeak, we know no more than we did when we contacted you over six hours ago about why the collision alarms sounded," a Timossi tracer said over open air to the Timossi Commander of the three stations. The tracer paced back and forth in his tiny office, which he and his officers shared on the dark side of the *Clea*. Running his fingers through his thinning blond hair, he chewed at a cuticle on his left thumb and stared at the communication screen that took up the entire right side of his office.

"We've heard unconfirmed reports of two deaths in the observation tower. Sir, you know that the military doesn't want us here. They have not shared any information. We are reporting on what we've learned from passers by and from reports from ships queuing to dock," a young woman said, as she stepped into the viewing screen's focus then stepped back behind the outpost commander. "All the ships are being kept beyond the Carpenter Barrier, a half million miles away."

"Sir, I've just learned that another body, that of a sailor from the Tapia ship, the *Yrr*, has been found in the ship's reactor room. She was also out of uniform and has turned to dust. Her identification tag gives her name as 00-2-477. She was reactor personnel and should have been wearing pink. She was found—or what was left of her—was found in a white uniform. This out-of-uniform state seems to have a lot of significance here with the Tapias," the commander said, as he placed a holographic image into the viewing screen. A fuzzy picture was relayed to Timossi headquarters in Tanzania, informing personnel of the Tapias' deaths and false alarms. Then messages of other strange deaths began arriving from the *Bole* and the *Galileo*.

Regaining consciousness, Captain Kalt and Plas inspected the crew, who were still in deep hibernation.

"The crew's bodies are still iridescent, calm. They have not been disturbed," Plas began. He stopped and looked in the direction of the cloudy planet and joined Kalt at the viewing screen.

"What do you make of that?" she asked. "The objects are about..." consulting her sextant she continued, "about five million miles. Do you see the faint outlines of... of... three crescent moons?"

"Yes," he answered, frozen for a minute in front of the viewing screen.

"I have not seen anything like these moons. They are huge, 2000-3000 times larger than our ship," he continued, the air turning dark maroon with awe.

"Look, there. There are viewing docks, and small pod things reflecting pale sunlight. It appears as if someone or something has created three artificial moons which orbit the cloudy planet." Kalt said, tinges of maroon surrounding her.

Putting up her hand and turning to Plas, she said, "Listen to the audio signals vibrating in the air. Do you hear voices coming from the strange objects?"

"No, I hear nothing."

"There's something there; very faint, coarse, and unintelligible, definitely not the melodic tones to which we are accustomed. Perhaps there are beings out there that can help us," she said, as she looked at the rapidly growing moons that in seconds filled her viewing screen.

Chapter 2

Jamaica Wong, a member of the Timossi Interplanetary police force, just completed her rookie year as a tracer, or police detective, where she worked as back-up personnel in the mining wars on Earth's moon and back-up in the Saari Plea negotiations on Saturn. She was assigned to the homicide division. Many Earth college graduates just beginning their ten years of volunteer service chose police, government or medical research. Jamaica chose the police force as a tribute to her African American grandfather, Balthazar Ballon. Now, like most second year detectives she wanted to work in the badlands of Uranus, which resembled the Earth Old West of the 1870s.

Jamaica rose from her chair and answered her halovision while pacing on her houseboat, moored in the Sacramento River.

"Good morning Jamaica. I know that you're anxious to find out about your next assignment," Wilson Gomez, Jamaica Wong's first line supervisor said, as he walked around his massive redwood desk at Timossi headquarters. Not waiting for a response he continued, "You've been assigned to the *Galileo*, for, at least, the next six months."

"The *Galileo*, then you weren't able to convince the Chancellor to let me go to *Er*?" she asked.

"I tried. I thought I had him convinced when McPeak called and asked for you."

"McPeak? Me, what's going on?"

"You probably know more than I," Wilson answered sarcastically, an edge of envy creeping into his voice.

Recovering, he stroked his graying beard and continued, "Sorry, I didn't mean that. I'm just a little tired. I've heard some good things about the *Galileo*. You should enjoy it there. Besides, you can take your vacation on *Er*. There will still be bad guys to find."

"I guess," she said, with a loud sigh.

"Oh by the way you'll have back-up. Neils will meet you on the *Galileo*."

"Great, now I need a baby sitter for a stupid space station. I'll need to tell Andrew and my parents about this latest turn of events," she added, as if an afterthought.

"Andrew won't like it."

"No, he won't," she replied as she looked up into the halovision and into Wilson's cold dark eyes. Jamaica broke the connection and turned to look out at the clear warm afternoon. She punched in her parent's halovision code and waited. Her earlier piano lesson long forgotten with all the morning interruptions, Jamaica absently unfolded a pale blue silk runner and placed it on top of the closed baby grand. She remembered with a smile her Grandmother Wong's horror on her first visit to the houseboat, a few years prior, to find the runner, an antique 19th Century piece being used as a throw for the piano, or worse, on the back of an equally ancient rocker. Still smiling to herself, Jamaica remembered the conversation she and her grandmother had then.

"Grams, what's the use of having nice things if they're always in trunks? I want to enjoy all of my collections. With me just beginning service as a tracer, you know I might not come back from my assignment. Then who'd enjoy all this?"

She swept her arms around the jade, coral and mahogany art pieces the family had given her over the years. The rest of the barge/houseboat was as filled as the chart room, with African sculptures, Native American baskets and Martian crystal vases, as well as carved Venusian snow rocks. Tia Chung Wong tried not to think of the nine more years of public service that lay ahead for her favorite granddaughter. *Of all the volunteer organizations Jamaica could have chosen, why had she followed her*

American grandfather when she would have made a wonderful anthropologist like her mother? Her superior analytical thought processes would serve both occupations well.

Emerging from her daydream, Jamaica spoke into the halovision recorder.

"Dad, Mom—hi, I'm coming to dinner. I'm bringing food, chicken salad and green tea." Taking a deep breath, Jamaica looked up the halovision numbers for both sets of grandparents and her boy friend, Andrew.

"I better call Andrew first. He's going to be upset."

###

"Hi, Andrew," Jamaica said when he answered his halovision call. He looked up from his flashdisc-covered table and smiled. He pushed some flashdiscs to the middle of the table and sat on the table's edge. Jamaica was seated in the middle of her large oatmeal colored sofa. It was her only concession to the rest of her family. The sofa, usually covered with police reports or music audioscopes, was wide enough for her father's 6'3" frame. At 5'2" Jamaica looked much younger than her 25 years when seated back in the middle of the colorful throw pillows. Today, the image was complete as she nibbled her right thumbnail and chose her next words with care.

"Hi, Jamaica. What a nice surprise. I thought you were going to visit your Chinese grandmother. Is she going to join us for the *Othello* opening?"

"No, she won't be coming and I can't either. I'm leaving tomorrow for the *Galileo*."

"The *Galileo?* You promised that you'd attend *Othello* with me."

"I told you I have to leave tomorrow. For some reason, McPeak wants me on the next flight."

"McPeak? Can't he find someone else to solve a murder for once?"

"I didn't say anything about a murder. He wants me on the *Galileo*."

"You're just a second year tracer. McPeak only calls newcomers when there is a serious murder somewhere."

"You're not attractive when you whine. This conversation is ridiculous. I don't know what he wants anymore than you do. He asked for me. I'm going. Maybe he wants me to do research on some old Earth murder files, far away from distraction."

"So, I'm a distraction."

"Andrew, I… Oh forget it. Yes, you're a distraction. I'm leaving for the *Galileo*."

Jamaica, her face hot with anger, broke the halovision connection.

Walking topside and speaking to herself, a habit she'd had since childhood, she scolded, "Jerk, he knew that I was going to spend my volunteer years in the Timossi. He's getting too possessive. Well, I'm leaving and I'm going to have a good time even if I die of boredom."

She threw a handful of bread crumbs from the duck feeder hidden in one of the boat's side panels to a gaggle of ducks paddling in the river off the port bow.

Sighing, Jamaica punched in the next set of numbers.

"Hello Gramama, is Pop Pop around?" Jamaica asked as the image of Kaila, her African American grandmother, came into view.

"Hello Jamaica. Yes, Batz is in the garden," she replied, referring to her husband by his nickname.

Kaila was dressed in a yellow linen and dandelion fabric sleeveless pants suit. The color complemented her light tan skin. Her wavy jet-black hair was cut short and framed her small, wrinkle-free face. Jamaica wore her hair cut in the same style as Kaila who looked closer to 45 than her 73 years. Human life expectancy currently averaged 165 years.

"I swear I don't know what he did with his time before he retired from the Timossi. Cross-breeding exotic plants with our Shasta Daisies are taking almost as much time as when he was on the force. He spends almost every waking moment fiddling around in the dirt."

Kaila Ballon smiled, and turning from the halovision

screen, she called, "Batz, honey, come into the house. Jamaica's calling."

A few seconds later a tall, wiry dark brown man with a full head of salt and pepper curly hair appeared and stood next to the short woman who'd been his wife for 50 years. He was wearing muddy denim pants and a light blue cotton shirt under a green and gray sweater that was covered in holes.

"Pop Pop, are you still wearing that old sweater? The only things holding it together are the holes."

"This is my favorite round the house sweater. Did you call just to ball me out about my clothing?" Batz said, trying to hide the smile in his voice.

"No, I wanted you and Gramama to know I'll be leaving for the *Galileo* tomorrow."

"The *Galileo,* how wonderful! I want to take Kaila there for our next anniversary!" Batz interrupted.

"You're the only one who's excited about me going."

"I think it's wonderful. Batz has told me so much about the rain forest and the species' breeding colony that I can hardly wait to go. Be sure to call us every chance you get," Kaila said.

Jamaica realized any help she thought she would get from her grandparents in support of her quest for assignment to the outer planets was lost. She spent the next half hour listening to stories about Mount Shasta, California, her grandparent's hometown, which after years of decline was growing once again with a population of nearly 2,000. Batz, a retired tracer and budding botanist, and Kaila, a retired astrophysicist, loved the quiet small town feel of Mount Shasta, which basked in the shadow of the sacred mountain from which the town took its name.

Jamaica walked into her galley and looked around the teak cabinets. She absently touched the smooth surface as she prepared a strong pot of tea. A few minutes later, after settling back into the sofa's cozy comfort, she called her Chinese grandparents.

"Grams Tia-Chung, how wonderful you look," Jamaica said, as her grandmother's image appeared in the halovision screen.

"Jamaica dear, how nice to see you. You did receive my halogram that Sui-Kai and I are attending the opera in Guilan, in old Iran and cannot make it to Sacramento? We'll visit with you and Andrew the next time we're in California."

"Yes, thanks Grams. I received your message. I called to let you know I've been assigned to the *Galileo*. I don't know when I'll be back home, maybe in six months. Where's Grandfather?"

"The *Galileo*, I often wondered what the sunset there would be like," Tia Chung interrupted. "Sui-Kai's in his study. He's busy with his models of the Three Kingdoms' massacre. He never hears the halovision when he's in the study. He probably has it turned off."

Tia-Chung, a year younger than Kaila, wore her long, black hair in a bun at the nape of her neck. Her face, lined and wrinkled after years of working in the sun, made her appear older. She was a universally renowned watercolorist. Most of her works captured the plains and mood of northern China, as centuries earlier Georgia O'Keefe captured the moods of New Mexico. Tia Chung preferred to dress in the traditional pantsuits of the rural Chinese farmers; that day she was wearing a pale peach colored silk blouse and wide-legged oatmeal fabric pants.

"Kai, turn on the halovision, Jamaica's calling. She's going to the *Galileo*," Tia-Chung shouted.

Looking up from the small figure he was painting, a miniature of General Yuan Shao's favorite horse, Sui-Kai laid the still wet figure on a drying stand and waved at Jamaica's image. She waved back, took a sip of tea, and looked at the dual halovision screens in her Chinese grandparent's home.

"The *Galileo*, huh, never cared much for space stations. Now if you can find a way to time travel back to the ninth century China, then I'd join you. I don't know if these colors are correct."

"How long are you going to be gone?" Sui-Kai picked up a

dry figure and turned it over in his right hand, then placed it back in the middle of the battlefield he'd constructed on his study table.

"I don't know, six months maybe. Don't you know anyone who can get me assigned to one of the outer planets? That's where the action is."

"Ah so that's why the call. I thought you might miss your old grandparents, instead it's a favor," Sui-Kai replied softly.

"I do miss you both. It's just... well, I want to go to the outer planets. Space stations are boring. How am I going to use my analytical skills on a space station?"

"I could call McPeak."

"He's the one who wants me on the *Galileo*."

"Then that's where you're going. What did Batz have to say?"

"Same as you."

"Ah well, enjoy the *Galileo*." Never one to mince words, Sui-Kai got up from the hard back chair on which he was seated, stretched his back and took a sip of water from a glass at his right. He was tall and dark like many northern Chinese but his most remarkable feature, besides his height of 6'3", was his green eyes. While Jamaica resembled her African-American grandmother, she inherited her Chinese grandfather's dark green eyes, right down to the epicanthic fold.

Knowing the four people she called on for support were all excited about her new assignment, Jamaica sighed as she looked over Sui-Kai's battlefield. With a feeling of resignation, she spent the next ten minutes talking about Triton paints she would bring back for both of the grandparents. After disconnecting from her China call and looking around her cozy home Jamaica got ready to visit her parents.

When Jamaica arrived at her parents' home near 5:30 p.m. she saw her father Xi Sung's yellow, dented hovercraft and an unfamiliar cherry red craft parked on the family pod. She pulled in behind her father's vehicle and walked inside the large two-story Spanish villa that had been her home as a child. Hearing voices coming from her father's study, she walked closer to the door, where her ears were assaulted by the twangy, nasal tones of a singer.

"Gosh, what is Daddy listening to?" she asked aloud as she walked past the study to the kitchen and placed a salad in the refrigerator. When she walked back to the study and opened the door, neither her father nor the young man with him heard her enter. Both sat, eyes closed, with their hands resting on their flat stomachs as they lay on comfortable matching light tan leather loungers and listened to the lyrics of the song. A glass of brandy sat on low tables near each chair.

"Lily was a princess, she was fair-skinned
and precious as a child,
She did whatever she had to do, She had
that certain flash every time she smiled.
She'd come away from a broken home, had
lots of strange affairs.
With men in every walk of life which took
her everywhere.
But she'd never met anyone quite like the
Jack of Hearts...."

Jamaica moved closer to her father, who sensing her presence, opened his eyes and gestured for her to sit down on the pillow-laden love seat beneath the open window. She tiptoed past the young stranger visiting her father.

"Ah, Jamaica dear, I got your message. Hillary will be very pleased to see you. I am hoping that she returns today. I want you to meet Christian Sokoto, a colleague from Marshall Elementary School," Xi Sung said.

Christian got up from the lounger. His six-foot eight-inch frame dwarfed her and her six-foot-tall father. Christian extended his hand and clasped Jamaica's firmly. His warm smile lit up his face, causing his dark eyes to sparkle with mischief.

"Pleased to meet you, Jamaica, I've heard a lot about your adventures on the moon," he said in a strong, rich baritone voice.

"Thanks."

"You caught us listening to an old Bob Dylan recreation of *Lily, Rosemary* and *The Jack Of Hearts.*"

Jamaica turned to her father.

"Bob Dylan? I never heard of him," she said as she moved away from Christian while giving her father a friendly hug.

"Go ahead, Son, tell her all about your favorite poet."

"Bob Dylan was one of two or three of the great 20th Century poets, composers and musicians. Quincy Jones was another great musician. Quincy was a genius with music and Dylan a master poet. Dylan is probably better known as a poet. I teach 20th and 21st Century music history. My specialty is classic rock-and-roll and jazz," Christian said, sitting back into the lounger.

"I have an audioscope cover I can show you," he said, as he fumbled through stacks of flashdisc covers that lay near his feet on the blue Chinese rug.

"I enjoy the new classics myself. Particularly Jung Jamieson and Martinez Jones. Is that Dylan's real voice?"

"Yes. As you know, engineers perfected the audio chip in the late 20^{th}century to where we today can hear all the old 20th century singers in their own voices," Christian replied.

Oh, a real teacher. Now he'll probably tell me more than I ever wanted to know about old music, she thought, as she got up and moved toward the door.

"He sure had a strange voice," Turning and facing Christian, Jamaica said, "it's nice to meet you."

"Dad, when's Mom due home?"

"She should be here any minute. We'll be right out. I want to hear the rest of the audioscope," Xi Sung said. Leaning over, he turned the audioscope higher. Jamaica closed the study door and returned to the kitchen. She listened to the music, but she did not hear the words.

###

"Hi, Mom. Where have you two been?" Jamaica asked as Hillary and her ever-present Jeeves 321, Kofi, entered the house from the backyard. Both were covered in dust from head to foot.

"Oh hello, dear. Are you staying for dinner or just dropping by?" Hillary asked. She attached the vacuum pump, just inside the mud-room, to the robot. She stripped off her clothing and stepped into the shower across from the robot's vacuum pump. Hillary wrapped her hair in a shower net cap.

"Just dropping by," Jamaica answered.

"That's nice. Kofi and I have been exploring an old roadway in Pueblo Bonito for the past three weeks. We've found some more evidence that the roadway and the Nasca Lines had the same purpose. I'm meeting with Jonathan Truman from Berkeley…" The rest of her words were lost in the noise of the shower water and the robot's vacuum. Jamaica returned to the kitchen and prepared a cup of hot green tea for herself and her mother.

Beads of water glistened among the glass and ceramic beads in Hillary's entwined thick dark coils as she toweled her hair dry and walked into the kitchen. She took a seat across from Jamaica at the large apple-red wooden table. She wrapped one of Xi Sung's large white terry-cloth bathrobes closer around herself and asked,

"So what's wrong?"

"Wrong? Does something have to be wrong for me to come and see you?" Jamaica asked, taking a sip of tea.

"No, but you only prepare Grandmother Wong's green tea when you're upset. Is it something to do with the Timossi?"

"I've been assigned to the *Galileo* for the next six months. Andrew, the jerk, is being a complete ass just because I'm going there."

"Um... the *Galileo*—is there trouble there? Why would anyone send a homicide detective to a space station?"

"That's what Andrew and I argued about. McPeak asked for me himself."

"McPeak? Honey, this assignment may be more dangerous

than you think."

"Mom, I'll be fine. If there is trouble, well that's why I joined the Timossi. To bring in the bad guys."

"Yeah, to bring in the bad guys, what have you been doing, digging around mines looking for smugglers, that's what. McPeak's people are old fashioned homicide investigators."

"Mom, the *Galileo* isn't the twenty third ring of Uranus. It's not outlaw territory. It's a dull boring space station where I'll probably spend six months doing paper work. More than likely putting years of McPeak's unsolved murders into some type of system so he can reminisce during his dotage. What else could possibly happen out there?"

"I don't know. I have an uneasy feeling about this assignment."

"Mother, you're not going to start that old *I have a feeling stuff*, are you?"

"Laugh all you want. Something is going on there and it isn't paper work. Mark my words."

"Mom, it's just like any other small city that's a thirty-year-old orbiting space station. I don't think it has more than 2,500 earth personnel on it. All that space—it's about the size of our moon, so few people. There are not enough people to keep one tracer busy. And to make matters worse, I'm going to have back-up."

"Back-up?"

"Because of the Tolo incident, gosh, I wish I were going to *Er* or the Twenty-third."

"Who lives there?" Hillary asked as she looked past her daughter to the hall leading to Xi Sung's study.

"Where?"

"The *Galileo*."

"Mostly scientists, engineers, teachers some researchers and their dependents. Most of the scientists work in solar engineering and solar research."

"I would guess so. Pretty darn close to the sun." Hillary took a sip of her tea and a bite of cookie from the plate in front of her. Jamaica looked out the window.

"Are you going to tell me why you really came by?"

"I told you, I'm going to the *Galileo*. Did you know that there's a duplicate of the Amazon basin on the seventieth through ninety-second floors?"

"No, I didn't. Why don't you stay for dinner and you can tell your father all about your new assignment. Speaking of your father, what is that noise?" Hillary asked, turning toward loud sounds coming from the study.

"Daddy and a co-worker are in the study. They're listening to the strangest music I've ever heard. Rock and roll, really old stuff. Daddy's friend says the oddest things. I've read most of the classics and I never heard of Bob Dylan or Quincy Jones." Jamaica made a face, shook her head and took another sip of the now tepid tea. She sat back in the chair.

"Are you going to tell me about Andrew?"

"Andrew... uh... you know he's never liked the idea that my years of service would be to the Timossi; like there's something dangerous about working in homicide. He has such a twenty-first century notion of women. You'd think that with him being an attorney and all that he'd..." Jamaica took another drink of the tea and continued speaking.

"You'd think that he'd know me by now. We've known each other all our lives. When we fell... uh... I mean, when our relationship changed."

"Dear, your father and I know that you and Andrew love each other very much. You've never been shy about telling me anything. Don't think that because you're a homicide detective that you're going to start now. Let me warm up the tea water." Hillary gathered the three sizes too large bathrobe close to her body as she stood up and put the tea kettle on the natural gas stove.

Jamaica, a hint of anger returning to her voice, answered. "We were both surprised at the intensity and depth of our feelings for each other. I know we should have known that the romance was doomed from the beginning. We're too much alike. Everyone knew it; all our friends, you and Dad, his folks, everyone. I just know that last year was the happiest I've ever had. I am going to miss him."

"Will you need me to start supper?" Kofi asked, walking into the kitchen and moving the tea kettle to the back burner.

"Not yet Kofi, see if Xi Sung and his guest want anything. Jamaica and I have a lot to discuss."

"Yes, Hillary." Jamaica and Hillary turned toward him and waited until he walked out and shut the door.

"Go on dear."

"I really like Andrew. It's sweet that he's old fashioned. This is the first time that his old fashioned ideas affected my work. I used to like the way he thought. How he'd argue as he played the role of the devil's advocate. He used to tell me that he believed the devil's advocate was his favorite vantage point because to do well you had to be absolutely convincing on both sides. I always thought that he would make an excellent defense attorney."

"Defense? Isn't he a prosecutor?"

"Yes, for the past four years."

"So what happened this morning?"

"Mother, he was furious—absolutely furious that I won't quit the Timossi and be... and be his ornament at art openings and the opera, or whatever. He was charmed to be seen with a tracer, during my rookie year. He's been resenting my work lately. I didn't pay that much attention to how much he was complaining. I know that he was making up excuses for me. He doesn't have to be ashamed that I'm in law enforcement. It's an excellent volunteer job. I love it."

The tea kettle whistled. Getting up, Jamaica poured fresh water on the tea leaves.

"Mom, I'm afraid that our relationship ended this morning. We said some really hateful things to each other."

"You could apologize."

"Me? He should apologize. I'm not going to."

That's what I thought. Both of them are too stubborn to say that they're sorry, Hillary thought. Taking her daughter's hand in hers, she patted it gently.

###

The audioscope ceased. The song finished.

"Well, what do you think of it?" Christian asked as he slipped the audiodisc into its container.

"Interesting. I'm not sure that Dylan's my kind of music. But I liked that piece. I really enjoy the Quincy Jones and The Branford Marsalis trio you've lent me. Let me keep this audiodisc for a while. I'll listen to the entire thing again, and then we'll discuss this some more." Looking out the window, Xi Sung saw Hillary's hovercraft.

"Hillary's home, can you stay for dinner?" he asked Christian, who was standing by the study door.

"No, some other time. I have to get to San Francisco. I have a date, later. I will go in to say hello to Hillary." They left the study and walked down the hall to the kitchen. Hillary, who had gone upstairs to dress, returned just as Xi Sung and Christian entered the kitchen.

"Hi, Honey," Xi Sung kissed her and said, "you remember Christian Sokoto." Xi Sung moved out of the way as Christian shook hands with her. Glancing at her father's friend, Jamaica noticed that he shook her mother's hands in the Senegalese fashion, with her hands cupped between his two.

How nice, she thought.

Smiling as they clasped hands, Hillary said, "Christian, you're my favorite of Xi Sung's friends. Even though your taste in music is a little… how should I say it… exotic?"

"Not as exotic as you."

"Flattery will get you very far, my dear." They laughed and hugged each other like old friends.

"Xi Sung invited me to dinner. Sorry I can't stay. Perhaps some other time, Miss Wong. Nice to meet you." Nodding to Jamaica as he took his coat from Kofi, Christian walked with Xi Sung to the front door.

###

"'Mimai, tell your old dad about the *Galileo*. It's the blue square, isn't it?" Xi Sung asked, calling Jamaica by her pet name as the family sat down to supper.

"Dad, you know the *Clea* is the blue cube. Want me to tell you about it?"

"Sure. Pass the salad while you're at it. You can't expect a starving father to listen on an empty stomach."

"Here," Jamaica said, handing the grapefruit and avocado salad across the table. "The *Clea*, at least what we've been told in class, is a state of the art military station of about 2,000 Tapia soldiers."

"How big it is? Twice as big as our moon, isn't it?"

"Yes, it's the biggest artificial satellite around Vos. The soldiers receive hazard pay because it's so close to the sun. Tapias have trouble with the concept of light engineering, or so I've been told."

"I've heard that bright sunlight has sent some Naresh personnel mad," Hillary interjected.

"Bright sunlight must be a very difficult concept to describe to the folks back home who only know perpetual twilight," Xi Sung said, adding an extra drop of honey onto his wheat toast.

"I've seen pictures of the interior. It's the brightest station with colorful yellow walls and orange air supply lines. Even the floors are painted in shades of lavender with murals of ancient Tapia battles. The soldier's uniforms are colored to reflect their duty. Can you believe that? Ugh, having to wear the same color every day for years. No wonder they go mad," Jamaica said, adjusting her powder blue cat tail fabric dress.

"Everyone finished? I'll pick up the dishes," she said, after an hour of small talk, scooting her chair from the mahogany dining room table.

"Did she say anything to us about Andrew?" Xi Sung asked, as soon as the dining room door closed behind her.

"No. Just because they've had a little fight doesn't mean that we can't invite him over. Besides, you two have been playing chess once a month since he was seven years old.

There's no need to stop now."

"Six months is a long time. They'll make up. They always have," Hillary said, getting up, blowing out the candles and walking arm-in-arm with Xi Sung, into the living room.

"Mom, Dad, I didn't realize how long we'd talked. I can't stay for dessert. I have to get an early start tomorrow. Neils and I are leaving on the 0630 time traveler, and I need my rest. Besides, I can see that you two old married folks want to be alone."

"Well, Hillary has been on her archaeological dig for three weeks. Normally, I would have come to see her, since she was so close. But I was busy with a research paper, which was due yesterday."

"And as usual, he delivered it to the government office at 16:30, just before they closed," Hillary said, giving Xi Sung an extra hug.

"I love you both. Don't worry about me. The *Galileo* is quiet and harmless. I won't die, unless it's from boredom. See you in six months. I'll call with my halovision number when I arrive."

"I hate packing for extended assignments. I even failed to program the Jeeves 322 properly, poor thing packs as poorly as I do. Where did I put my toothbrush?" Neils Daliz said to himself, combing his long blond hair into his familiar and non-regulation ponytail, and gazing at his reflection in the steamy mirror. He clasped the gathered hair with a knotted leather rope from which hung clear glass volcanic beads from Ou. Stroking the beard he'd grown while on Er, he smiled.

"May not be regulation but I like it and Hannah likes it," he said, running his long, heavy fingers down his beard and throat.

"I better hurry if I'm going to make the time traveler. Jamaica hates waiting for me, but she always holds the vehicles until I arrive. One day, my boy, she won't. I can't stand here talking to the mirror forever." He turned around in the large dark blue tile bathroom and completed getting dressed, putting on a regulation dark brown tracer suit, and knee boots.

Stepping outside onto the balcony of his condominium to gaze at his obscured view, through the dense morning fog of downtown San Francisco and the bay beyond, Neils glanced over at his sleeping wife, Hannah.

"I wish I could join you once again," he whispered, leaning over and kissing her shoulder.

The silver Coptic cross he had given her as a birthday present, which lay across the back of her neck, caught the light from the bathroom lamp, glowed brightly and shimmered in contrast to her dark, almond-colored skin. Her tiny, nearly 95-pound body barely caused a ripple among the tossed sheets and pillows on the huge king-sized bed. Murmuring something incoherent in her sleep, she turned to expose her small left breast as the top ice blue cotton sheet pulled from her body. Pulling the sheet over her, he left the bedroom, closed the door behind him and walked into the kitchen in silence.

"Let her sleep a few minutes longer," he said to himself.

"Damn, I've picked up Jamaica's annoying habit of speaking to myself," he said, making a fresh pot of Kona coffee.

"This aroma will wake Hannah in a few minutes."

He walked over to the cage of Hannah's yellow-naped Amazon parrot, removed the night covering from it and said, "Good Morning, No Pi L." Neils stroked the bird's feathers and handed him a graham cracker.

"How's Hannah's gifted student today?"

"Cracker."

"Cracker, huh? No wonder you no longer resemble the small bundle of green feathers you were nine years ago. If you keep eating like this, I'll have to buy a larger cage," Neils said, continuing the morning ritual he'd established with the parrot.

No Pi L, who was a very talented bird, responded at the level of a twelve-year-old human.

"Good Morning... beautiful day... warm..." the parrot said, nibbling at the second cracker. Opening the cage, Neils let out the beautiful 400-gram, full-grown green, yellow and blue, yellow-naped Amazon parrot.

"Thank you," No Pi L said, flying out of the cage to his perch, which was an iron coat rack in the shape of a seven-armed Saari sand dweller. The perch, the bird's favorite, was a house-warming gift from Hannah's sister.

Neils poured a cup of the fresh-made coffee and added cream and three sugars to a large green cup with a picture of a *Thane,* the multicolored striped wild animal of the Eron, which looks like a large earth tiger, on the side opposite the handle. Taking a sip and frowning, he added another half-teaspoon of sugar. Turning to the sound of water running, he poured a second cup, this one black with no sugar, then he walked back into the bathroom. Hannah smiled at him, replaced her toothbrush and stepped into the bath. She stopped and turned to let him admire her body, and then with a smile, she blew kisses into the air.

"Stop it. I'm late for work as it is. No time for whatever you're planning," he said, smiling back at her and handing her the coffee.

"Good morning to you too," she said, easing down into the steaming water and reaching for the coffee. Taking a sip, she raised her face for a kiss as Neils knelt beside the bathtub. The kiss lingered on their lips. She splashed water in Neils' direction as he kissed her. He got up and left the bathroom.

Calling after him she said, "Call me and give me your number. No Pi L and I won't get to the *Galileo* for another three days."

"Okay." Neils looked around the living room and pat himself down. Satisfied that he had what he needed, he ran to the elevator and to the Time Traveler.

Chapter 3

The *ZIXC's* engines stopped about 10,000 miles from the large, bright object positioned off its starboard side. Surveying the damage caused by the intense winds, Kalt and Plas looked around at the broken, spilled and torn objects as the ship's robot maintenance crew cleaned up.

"It seems that the winds have stopped," Kalt said, stating the obvious.

"I believe that we are here," she continued, pointing out a large star cluster on the star map, on the edge of their known universe.

"We should be here," she pointed to another spot on the other side of the map.

"There must have been a force field or something which brought us to this windy place. I do not want to believe what I am feeling but the stars do not lie," Plas replied, as for a moment he glowed deep purple.

"The stars outside the viewing screen are not Geahan. We are in a strange place with strange winds. A mediocre sun and a planet, which has artificial moons," he continued.

"Worse yet, the planet seems to be one which our instruments cannot read," Kalt replied as she studied the static that greeted the atmospheric robot she had sent to the planet.

"It should have sent back readings immediately. What kind of place is this?"

"Have you sent a distress probe?"

"Yes."

"Perhaps you should send one with a wider arc. Send it to

where our five sister ships should be."

"Yes, where they should be."

The *Bole's* collision alarms rang again. The Vos scrambled to full alert, and scientists in the observation tower scanned the horizon yet saw nothing.

"Nothing is out there," a seasoned scientist said to her colleague, straightening up from the observation telescope.

"Our computers indicate that something is attacking the planet and the space stations. There must be something." She rubbed her eyes with her index fingers and peered once again into the calm dark sky.

"What happened?" a young ensign asked while stepping aside to let a Tapia commander enter the small control room near the *Clea's* observation tower.

"Go about your duties ensign. Speak to no one about what you have seen."

"I didn't see anything, Sir."

"That's right, you didn't see anything," the commander 00-4-29 said as he stepped over the white uniforms that belonged to the four ensigns who staffed the tower.

"Why were these ensigns out of uniform?" He asked no one, as he was alone, surrounded by dusty white uniforms.

The air supply continued to crystallize in the pumping stations but went unnoticed. One old computer clicked an alarm. The soldier nearest the computer hit it with his fist, moving the instrument readings back to normal.

"Obsolete machine, you should have been sent to the recycling center years ago," the soldier designated 0-86-1 said, giving the computer another unfriendly knock.

"Why am I stuck with this old junk? Back on Tapia we had the latest toys. These old computers, with the clicking and whirling of the bamboo shards should have been sold for scrap before I was born. Father paid a lot to get me out here. He'd be really angry if he knew I was surrounded with this obsolete, noisy old stuff." He walked past the noisiest machine, looked over the ancient dials and instruments and checked his chart. He sat in a sturdy iron chair, brushed dust from his pale pink uniform, took out a *tacqu*, a mouth instrument much like the earth harmonica, only sounding more like a cello, and played a melancholy song.

"The *Clea*—silent, clean, calm contrasts so much with busy, noisy and polluted Tapia that even these old machines make me feel at home," he said after the song ended.

"Feel at home? How can you feel at home? Tapia's shrouded in grays, blacks and the dark colors of a moon far from the sun. It's a place where suspicion and distrust is encouraged, fostered and rewarded," his office mate replied.

"You better be careful. The Commander has spies everywhere," 0-86-1 murmured.

"You liked *Clea's* cool pink titronium exterior? How can you feel at home when orbiting Vos on a space station, only 67.1 million miles from the sun?"

"I just do. Thoughts of home make me sad. I am not going to be happy to return to the dark world which is my future; even if she came with me," 0-86-1 said, turning toward a computer operator across the room who was outside hearing range.

"I've been noticing her for a while. She's very young. I wonder how she got enough credits to come here. She hasn't changed into her green observation suit. Maybe she has the day off."

"We haven't changed either."

"I must sp..." The rest of his words never left his mind. Instead he fell dead to the floor. It didn't matter to the computer operator or 0-86-1's vocal companion as they were also dead.

Chapter 4

Aboard the *Bole*, seven Vosian traders crystallized in a bar, Rick's Café, near the Xury pier.

"How many times do I have to repeat this?" Serene, the owner-bartender asked.

"At least one more time," a Vosian police officer replied. "A tracer needs to ask you questions."

"I've been talking to the cops for hours. Why is a tracer going to see me?"

"Seven Vose just died in an American bar," he replied.

"Cigarette?" A young red-haired, chubby tracer, holding out a package of hand rolled *Ern* blend cigarettes settled comfortably into the seat opposite Serene.

"Take one," she continued, her round dimpled face breaking into a friendly smile.

"Thanks. I haven't smoked in years. I used to think only outlaws smoked cigarettes. I still craved the stuff and I need to do something with my hands. This coffee," pointing to a cup of thick, black New American coffee, "isn't doing its job."

Serena inhaled deeply on the cigarette then burst into a violent fit of coughing. Tears streamed down her face. She blew her nose on a large green cy handkerchief, pushed back a fallen strand of dyed blue hair from her face and adjusted her Vosian shoulder veil.

"So what killed em? I tell ya. I was right there," she waved the cigarette in the direction of the nearly empty bar. The tracer sat listening.

"They were laughing and joking. They'd had a good trade;

bolts of beautiful pink silk." She paused for breath and glanced down at the tracer's identification badge.

"Mariah Fitzsimmons, third year, tracer, assignment Bole Outpost."

"Name's Serene. Folks use ta compliment me on my name. Said I lived up to it. Nothing ever rattled me. That is til this morning. I've seen lots of things. Trader fights, Neptunian grudge matches, even the Saari mating ritual. But this, I been on this station for nearly ten years. Had this place built just like Rick's Café in Casablanca, seen it a thousand times. This place's identical right down to the fringe on the lamp shades."

"Wasn't the bar in Casablanca called the American Bar?" Mariah asked.

"Yeah, not many folks know that. Rick's Café sounds more intriguing, don't you think?"

"Yeah. You said something about pink bolts."

"I wish I'd paid more attention. They came in, ordered Yoma Rum, talked among themselves then just crystallized right in front of me. Turned to crystal. I could see clear through em. Even their rum crystallized."

"Did anyone else see this?"

"Huh?"

"Was there anyone else in the bar when this happened?"

"Yes, the customers on both sides of them saw. Must have left, probably too drunk to be of much help by the time the cops... by the time the tracers came. They didn't want to be crystallized any more than me."

"Was any other customer affected?"

"No. They probably brought some disease with them. Where did they say they were from?" Frowning, Serene took a sip of cold coffee.

"They were laughing and joking. They'd had a good trade. I remember the beautiful pink silk. Thinking how good some of it would look on me." Serene's hands began trembling.

"Pink silk?" Mariah asked.

"Yeah, beautiful, soft color." Serena stood so that she could see the table where the bolts laid and gasped.

"It can't be. What happened to it?"

"What can't be? What happened to what?" Mariah asked, turning to a table on which lay bolts of pure white silk.

"Sit down, tell me again. What had the traders talked about before this... this happened?"

"Them bolts, they were pink," Serene restated in a small, barely audible voice.

"What do you mean they were pink?" Mariah asked, lighting a cigarette for herself. *This was going to be a long day,* she thought.

"Pink, you know, pink. They were bragging about how inexpensive they got em. I know pink when I see it. Those bolts were pink."

Serena looked into Mariah's cool brown eyes, inhaled deeply once more, then continued.

"You're a young woman, maybe twenty years younger than me. You probably think I'm a hysterical old woman. I'm not one for hysterics. The silk was pink. The traders had much of it wrapped around themselves as they sat right at that table. I know it was pink."

"Damn, damn, damn, doctors found a vaccine for the common cold over 200 years ago. And for this damn flu, nothing. Oh, Ms. O'Brien, the flu must run its full course. Well I'm sick of it. Sick of it."

Yelling into the halovision and taking a fresh handkerchief from the bureau drawer, Heather O'Brien sat down hard on her sparse sofa.

"BING...", the halovision rang, "Hello Heather."

"Good morning Sam. Sorry you got me in a grumpy mood. I'm sick of being sick. I've been on the *Galileo* for a month and ill for the past week. I'm bored silly."

"You won't stay bored with these assignments. Shall I send over hard copies?" Sam replied.

"No. Halovision copies are fine." Looking around her

spacious 2,000 square foot apartment and holding her pink robe closed over her pink pajamas, she continued.

"Did you know that I'd asked for a replica of the Arizona desert as my internal view scape? Sometimes, Sam, I just need a break from the bright greens and colors of the forest once I return home. People probably think it strange, me being the chief environmentalist for the Amazon Avian labs. Don't mind me. I've been babbling to myself all morning. I was yelling at the halovision just before you called." She continued her nearly one-sided conversation with her co-worker as she walked to the internal window and picked up a cup of steaming chicken soup.

"The view is beautiful. I have it on random select. I never know what my mornings are going to look like. Just like on Earth. Sometimes I..." the rest of her sentence ended in a scream. Sam observed a bright flash followed by flames and called the medics. When the tracers arrived, it took two minutes for them to get Heather's address from the frightened and grieving Sam, who bordered on hysteria.

"What is happening? This is the fifth call we've had this morning. All the victims burned to death," said a young medic who covered Heather's body with a crocheted afghan taken from the sofa.

"Let the tracers handle it. They're at the hospital interviewing witnesses, attempting to interview survivors, checking clothing, work history, friends and family, looking for a common link. Many, like Ms. O'Brien, were alone, at home, when the 'accident' occurred," her companion replied with a shudder.

Chapter 5

Two Tracers returning to the *Galileo*, Olsen and McDonald, accompanied Jamaica and Neils aboard the time traveler, the *Kansas Maru*, when the halovision toned.

"Two ensigns assigned to the *Clea* have died under unusual circumstances," the mechanical voice of the news reader reported.

Stopping his solitary game of zi, the only Tapia aboard the *Kansas Maru* began a loud chant.

"What is happening?" Jamaica asked.

"He's into the death dirge. It is a familiar ritual for those of us who sail within Naresh's orbit. He must have sensed the deaths before the news report. He has been agitated for some time. Whenever a Tapia dies, except in battle, in order for his/her spirit to be healed, all other Tapias within space-sense must begin a mourning dirge. Tapias believe that they must be buried in Tapia soil for the spirit of healing to be complete," Neils replied.

"We better see the captain in case tracers are needed here. Deaths on space stations, unusual or not, fall under the purview of the Timossi," Olsen added.

Moving out of earshot of the Tapia the foursome hastened to the Captain's chambers.

"The initial communiqué spoke only of the two deaths in the observation tower on the *Clea* and the collision alarms that malfunctioned at the same time," Olsen continued.

"Wait, listen."

"Deaths aboard the *Bole* and the *Galileo* are confirmed. All three space stations' collision alarms sounded at the same time," The mechanical voice reported.

"The Captain wants to see you in the security pod," said a sailor who led the way for the tracers.

"The captain has already activated the ship to warp speed. We would arrive at the *Galileo* in an hour," the sailor continued.

###

"McPeak will brief us as soon as we reach the security pod," Neils said.

"McPeak has been the coordinating tracer, Second Grade, for the past six years on the *Galileo*," Olsen said as he walked next to Jamaica.

"McDonald and I've worked closely with him for a few very scary projects."

"Scary projects?" Jamaica asked.

"Not on the *Galileo*. It's very quiet, almost boring. I'm going on my way back to Ou after a short holiday. Space stations are too tame. McPeak likes to play tough. Don't let his gruff manner put you off. He's the best."

"Why'd you join the force?"

"I like working alone. There's a lot of space and a lot of bad guys out there. McPeak and I were born four centuries too late," Olsen replied, running his fingers though his coarse, crew cut black hair and fingering an ugly scar that crossed his left cheek just under his eye and ended near his chin.

"I see two old bounty hunters from the old West," Jamaica said with a smile. They entered the security pod and looked up into the huge red face of Aristotle McPeak, their leader. He was in mid-sentence.

"The information that we've received from the *Bole* and the *Clea* indicates that eleven beings have died within a very short time since the station's collision alarms sounded.

"All three stations are now on full alert. No one could see anything. None of the stations have been hit yet, but the computers indicate that there is something out there. We don't have anyone on the *Clea* yet. The Naresh military appear to be cooperating fully. Sorry I don't have more information to tell you. I'll meet you at dock Seven in a few minutes.

"Round the clock investigations will begin the minute the *Kansas Maru* docks. So I guess we'd better get started," McDonald said, tucking her fine, long blue-black hair under her tracer helmet and adjusting her laser pellet belt cartridge.

The *Kansas Maru* glided into a narrow dock on the *Bole* side of the *Galileo* and was met by McPeak.

"Come on to the hospital. Several burn victims are being treated there." McPeak led the four tracers through customs.

"They're all burned pretty badly. I'm surprised any are still alive," McPeak continued in a stage whisper.

"They've been covered in the new Juarez material."

"Juarez? Dr. Juarez is my mentor. We, some of his students, worked with him on the materials. I hadn't had an opportunity to see the product used in practice. Dr. Juarez is one of the Timossi's brightest scientists. He's been working on a non-allergenic, fireproof, medicinal material for nearly four years. He's only tested his product on prisoners in Earth's maximum-security prisons. This material is having remarkable side effects in calming prisoners and is just beginning to be used for burn victims," Jamaica said, her voice filled with awe.

"Dr. Juarez has just begun developing a more powerful vaccine for the most violent prisoners. He has not published his new theories in the medical journals. The *Galileo* is glad to be among the earliest recipients of the new Juarez material. The doctors are delighted and a little scared now that they are putting this 'wonder' material to use so quickly," McPeak replied.

"The station just received a small supply of Juarez a week ago. I sure hope it saved them. They're all too ill to be questioned. Brett and the others are still questioning coworkers, friends, anyone who was near the victims when it happened. I tell you, folks are scared," McPeak continued as he took a breath and wiped his perspiring brow. Standing to one side he let the new arrivals take their first sight of the victims.

"So far we can't find any common factor," he said with hesitation.

"These patient charts contain the victim's name, address, occupation, where the incident occurred, and what they were probably doing when it happened."

In an inner room of the crowded intensive care ward, three people lay covered in the green Juarez material.

"What's that odor?" McDonald asked as she wrinked her nose and held her hand over her mouth.

"It's *cy*, one of the main ingredients of the Juarez material. I'd heard that The World Health Organization and the Old America Drug Enforcement Agency have recently approved the use of the Juarez materials for severely burned persons," Jamaica replied.

"Takes your breath away when you're not expecting it."

"Yes, it has a very... hum... sharp odor," Jamaica replied. She turned toward McPeak and continued. "There must be something so obvious which links these people and the ones who've died that we're overlooking it."

A private smile crossed McPeak's face as he thought, *the reports of Jamaica Wong were indeed true. She is analytical and to the point.* He'd be very happy if she could solve this mystery so that folks could go back to living. At that moment the non-Timossi personnel of the three space ships were in a mild state of panic.

Bending over the bed of one of the victims, Jamaica looked at his name plate: Mark Kim, lab tech.

"It looks like he's too ill to speak or even point," she said while reviewing the briefing information handed to her: Kim, Mark; originally from New America, assigned to the *Galileo* five years earlier. Last visit to Earth was six months past. Married, one child, a son, Wills. Wife, Alana, also a lab tech.

"Where's his wife?" Jamaica asked.

"Mrs. Kim left the computer room for an early meeting immediately prior to the incident. She'd just changed from her lab uniform to her home clothes. I spoke to her earlier. She said that her husband didn't have any enemies. That he was well-liked. I sent her home. I think she's sedated. Her father's watching the boy," McPeak replied.

"How old is the boy?"

"Five... no, six. He hasn't been told much. You can question Mrs. Kim in a few hours after the sedative has worn off."

"The next person is Ms. Shirley Van Cale, a musician. The *Galileo* is her first space travel, other than the moon and the new Earth colonies. She's been on the *Galileo* for three days. Her traveling companion, Maria Smithson, also a musician, couldn't add anything to the preliminary investigation."

As they walked down the hall to the next victim's room, Olsen continued to read the briefing memo.

"She was going to stay on the *Galileo* once Ms. Van Cale's vacation ended. She doesn't want to get involved."

"Looks like she's involved whether she wants to be or not," McPeak replied.

"Yes, I guess so."

"She's to marry a time traveler pilot within a month. And was saving money. According to her statement she really doesn't know Ms. Van Cale. She agreed to be her roommate to save them money. They kept pretty much to themselves, rarely even sharing a meal."

"Really, why's that?" Jamaica asked.

"Let's see. Uh... Ms. Smithson is an early riser and Ms. Van Cale liked to sleep late."

"I'll speak to her again. McPeak, who interviewed her?" Olsen asked.

"Brett. Good guy, very thorough. I doubt if he missed anything."

"What else do we know about Ms. Van Cale?"

"She's from Old Europe, played first flute in the Royal Dutch Symphony for five years. She's unmarried, not dating anyone. At least not anyone steady. She was stricken after a bath. Ms. Smithson found her wrapped in a bath towel."

"Who do you have, McDonald?" McPeak asked, looking past Jamaica to McDonald, who leaned against the clean green wall and looked into her computer.

"Ms. Mapuha Smith-Brown. I know Ms. Smith-Brown very well. She's been useful to the Timossi in the past. She's not a snitch or an informant. But she's very well connected. Mapuha's a well-known prostitute who plies her trade on the time travelers or the *Rista* transport ships between planets. It's been a while since I've seen her."

"According to the customs report she arrived on the *Galileo* earlier this morning on the *Rista* vessel, *The Taino Clan*. The passengers, mostly elderly Saari, treated her like a wayward child. She made friends as easily with the old Saari as she had the young sailors whose ships she traveled. She was "struck" while walking on the tarmac after *The Taino Clan* docked."

"Coming down the tarmac?" Neils asked.

"That's what everyone said."

"Do we know how many male or female victims there are?" Jamaica asked.

"No. But I'll have the information soon," McPeak replied.

"What was Ms. Smith-Brown wearing?" Jamaica asked.

"Wearing? I don't know... let's see." McDonald punched a few buttons and scanned the small hand held viewer.

"Depending on who you talk to she was wearing either a pale pink or off-white Saari enki short dress when the ship docked. Some of the Saari said that Mapuha was dressed in pink. They added, I guess, a color that complemented her pale skin, as this information is highlighted. Others insisted that she was wearing white. She was in white when she arrived at the *Galileo* hospital," McDonald replied and turned the viewer off.

"We have to go to the morgue next, there are six bodies there. As you can see from the initial information no one seemed to know anyone else. They didn't have anything in common."

###

As he inspected the flamingo compound on the *Galileo's* thirtieth floor, the thoughts of zoo keeper Carl Starr were interrupted by a frantic call from his Jiangan assistant.

"The albino flamingos are dead," she said, her words rushing together sounded like *theablinoflamingosare* dead.

"Albino flamingos?" he replied. "We don't have any albino flamingos. Where are you?" he asked Morgan, the first-day-on-the-job Jiangan assistant, who had just completed her classes.

"The white ones, Sir, they're all dead."

"I'll be right there. Don't touch anything."

I wonder what has happened. We don't have any albino flamingos, he thought as he hurried to the zoo compound.

"My God, they are all dead," he exclaimed. He scrutinized the temperature module.

"It's 80 degrees. The birds were all young, the oldest only five years. When did they arrive?" He checked and rechecked the information in his log.

"They arrived from different zoos on Earth. They were Caribbean, as well as the Greater and Lesser Flamingos from Africa. There must an explanation, possibly a virus. They live 40-50 years, in captivity, on Earth. Morgan, prepare for an autopsy. We have to get to the bottom of this before whatever happened to these birds spreads to the others."

"Yes, sir," a tearful Morgan replied.

"I can't believe my eyes. It's as if their feathers had all aged. Or as if the color was drained. Don't worry Morgan, it wasn't anything you did or did not do. These birds must have brought a virus with them. I have to call Earth."

"Earth, sir?"

"I have to tell them not to send any more flamingos here. Not until we find out if there is something here which has caused these deaths, or something they brought with them. They appear to die from heat prostration."

"I checked the temperature. It was fine."

"I know, Morgan. I checked it myself a few minutes ago. It's the same reading I've gotten the last four times I checked."

###

Walking outside to her balcony, Jennifer Gonzales Smith-Ryan, the New America Ambassador to Vos, picked up a pot of her Pink Sisters, her prize geraniums.

"Darn, they don't do well here at all," she said to her Jeeves 322. She handed the dead plants to the robot for disposal. The deaths of the geraniums didn't register as something to be reported to the police.

Chapter 6

"I've confirmed that there are six bodies in the *Galileo's* morgue, ten in the *Clea's* and seventeen in the *Bole's*. Each station is conducting independent investigations as to the cause of the deaths of their inhabitants," McPeak said as he looked around the morgue.

"May I?" Jamaica motioned to inspect tissue and blood samples under the microscope.

"I've reviewed the Crime Scene Investigators' reports, searched charred clothing, scarred jewelry and other pieces of artifacts for information. I'm not getting anywhere. I don't see anything unusual here."

"Let's go to my office," McPeak suggested. "Perhaps there is something we've overlooked on the information flashdisc."

"How far is it?" Neils asked.

"Upstairs. It's on the floor above this one."

McPeak led the way upstairs to his office. It, like McPeak, was plain, no-nonsense. A Timossi issue desk, unadorned with anything personal, occupied the far wall near the inner windows. From his desk, McPeak could swivel around and view the daily comings and going of the *Galileo* personnel. A computer, a few flashdiscs and printouts, all Timossi issue, lay on the desk. An old-fashioned metal file cabinet, with the drawers part way opened stood to the right of the desk. A round, burl wood conference table dominated the rest of the room with four matching Timossi chairs placed around it. There were no pictures, paintings, art work, or clock on the walls. Pulling his chair from behind his desk, McPeak drew it up to the conference table. Jamaica, Neils Daliz, Olsen, and McDonald took seats around the table.

"You know McPeak, I can't remember the last time that I worked with another tracer. I mean, since my rookie year. It's kinda strange. I mean we're all..." McDonald started to glance around the table.

"We're all so used to going in, cleaning up the mess and getting out. A meeting with other tracers, I don't know if I can do it." She shook her dark hair then winked at Olsen.

"You'll have to get used to it. You two," pointing to Olsen then McDonald, "plus Mariah Fitzsimmons, are probably the most independent and strong-willed of a cadre of independent and strong-willed personnel anywhere. That's why I know you will work well with each other. Take a copy of the morning printout on the burn victims. Jamaica, summarize the material for the teams."

"Okay. Beginning in the order of discovery, the people are 1: Santana Collins, aged 62, widower, solar engineer, lives alone, a resident of the *Galileo* for twenty years. Four children all living on Earth; none connected with the *Galileo;* none in sensitive occupations."

"Anyone in his family involved with tracers?" Neils asked.

"Not really. He has six grandchildren, one Brazila, has been arrested twice for demonstrations against the New American colony on Earth's moon. She's currently serving time on Lunar II for blocking the entrance to the silver mines on Tranquility Base IV. School girl prank—she'll be out in two months. Mr. Collins' Jeeves 322 found him seated at the breakfast table. Neighbors heard him scream, and rushed to the Collins' household moments before the Jeeves found him. He died on route to the hospital. He was wearing a white dressing gown. Any questions?"

"No, go on, who's next?" Olsen asked.

"Number 2: Jane Harris, twenty-eight, married, grammar school professor on the *Galileo* on holiday with her husband, Kim-Yung Harris. Mr. Harris is an Earth oceanographer. This was their first visit to the *Galileo*. Jane Harris was shopping at

Aunt Lydia's Antique Shoppe when stricken. She'd gone into a dressing room to try on an antique-lace sleeping gown. Her screams brought the three sales staff to the dressing room but she was so badly burned that she died before the medics arrived. The sales staff needed to be sedated. All are in shock and have not yet given us any useful information."

"Was the husband there?" Olsen asked.

"No, Mr. Harris was at the bar in the Galileo Hilton when the incident occurred. The bartender and two regulars confirmed that he did not leave the bar during the two hours prior to and the hour after Mrs. Harris' death."

"Oh? How were they so sure?" McPeak asked, as he leaned forward and rested his elbows on the table.

"Kim Yung Harris is easily remembered because none of the bar regulars had ever met any of the blond Asians from New China."

"They are handsome," McDonald added with a smile.

"Victims three and four are Joan and Scott Buckley, two 18-year-olds, on their honeymoon aboard the *Galileo*. The kids told the hotel staff that both sets of parents were adamantly opposed to the marriage but reluctantly agreed when the kids ran away twice. They were very excited, as the trip to the *Galileo* was their first off planet Earth. They were found by the hotel robot-maid when the smoke detector went off and no one could get a response from them."

"I've notified the parents. They will arrive on the *Galileo* in three days. I dread taking them to the morgue for the formal identification," McPeak murmured.

"Number 5 is Joplin Darrow, aged 80, retired pediatrician. What's this? McPeak, the report states that Dr. Darrow died from a heart attack."

"I know. His body was burned seconds after death."

"After death?" the others echoed and approached the flashdisc in Jamaica's hand for a closer look.

"This says that Dr. Darrow was pruning his roses, Wendy's Pink Delight, a new bush he had just purchased through the Murphy seed catalogue, when he suffered his heart attack,"

Neils said as he handed the flashdisc to McDonald, who commented.

"He'd been anticipating the roses for over three months. It was all he spoke about, his widow, Mrs. Darrow, said."

"I'm going to see Mrs. Darrow later," Jamaica said. "Is this all of her statement?"

"Yes. Is there a clue?"

"I don't think so. She said, let me quote, 'the excitement of finally receiving the roses was too much for his heart. He'd been told by his doctor to take it easy. But he never listened to anyone's advice, except his own.'"

"Did she say anything about the burns?" McDonald asked.

"No, she couldn't explain them. She states that she was on the other side of the apartment when she heard him moan, then either he or she screamed. He kept saying 'the roses... the roses...' Let me see, what's this? Something about the color. What does this mean? The color?"

"Ask her to explain what she meant by color," McPeak replied.

"Okay. Do you want to see what's on the sixth flashdisc?"

"Please."

"This information is about George Hawkins. He's an attorney."

"George? I know him—knew him." Neils said. "He and I worked together during the Andromeda Conflict. I must say I'm surprised to hear he burned to death." The others in the room turned to face him and waited for him to continue.

"George drank a lot. He may have been an alcoholic. But he was also a brilliant debater. He and I became friends. We played polo on the Er grasslands and touch football on Earth."

"What else do you know about him?" McPeak asked.

"George lived alone. The *Galileo* was a resting place between cases. He loved the rain forest and would camp for weeks at a time deep within the 75th floor whenever he was trying to sober up. He was very fond of rum and always carried a filled silver flask."

"That makes some sense at least. According to this

flashdisc he was found on the 77th floor in the replication of the Peruvian river, the Ucayali. His boat was scorched. He'd been dead about an hour when found by a botanist. Mr. Hawkins' boat ran aground near a passenger entry port. His flask was empty."

"That's not surprising," Neils interrupted.

"Tiny crystal beads, the size of pin heads, were found fused to the boat's internal bottom. No one knows how he burned to death in the middle of a river," Jamaica continued.

"Let's go over these flashdiscs one by one," McPeak said, settling into a comfortable spot on his chair.

TONE, TONE, the halovision toned before they could begin.

"Hello, McPeak," Mariah Fitzsimmons said and nodded to the others in the room.

"Mariah, these are the tracers who will be helping me with this project. Jamaica Wong and Neils Daliz are new; you've met McDonald and Olsen before."

"Chief, there are 17 crystallized bodies here on the *Bole*. From what I've been able to gather so far all the men worked on the Vosian trading vessel, the *Calliope*. She's just returned from a four-month voyage to Naresh's moon, Galatea. The ship is still full of silks, perfumes, tobacco and spices. So far, I can't find anything which could have caused this phenomenon." Pausing, Mariah took a drink of coffee.

"You said that the men were all crystallized. Could you be more specific? I'm having trouble visualizing their condition," Jamaica asked, leaning forward toward the halovision. Her elbows rested on the conference table as she fiddled with the printouts before her. Everyone turned in unison and looked first at Jamaica then Mariah.

"Well, it looks like all the liquid in their bodies was frozen," Mariah explained. "The skin is 'papery and flaky' but hard as a rock. There's a shimmer to the skin which none of us can explain. The lighter-skinned Vose have a chalky-grey cast to the skin. The dark brown bodies resemble polished walnut. Its as if they were turned, instantly, into crystal statues. And you can see their internal organs."

"According to those in the bar it all happened very quickly, within seconds. I've sent a replicator and one body to the *Galileo's* morgue. It should arrive any minute. The *Bole's* morgue personnel have been unable to give me any directions.

"The Nore, our physican telepaths, are helping interview all the relatives. I could use some help from you guys. I'm on my way to the *Calliope* to interview the rest of the crew. Only the 17 who came to Rick's Café have been injured."

"Okay. Oh and Mariah, send me anything you find immediately. I'll contact the Nore, myself. No use duplicating the effort. We all want to find out what is behind this. I'll send Olsen here to meet you on the *Calliope*," McPeak said, and broke the connection.

Jamaica spoke first, "Tell us something about the Vose. I know their skin color is tan to dark brown, their blood is blue/green, iridium based. And they live in a caste system."

"They are the best traders in the universe," Olsen added.

"I know some of the Vose practice magic. What else do we know? Why only those men? Why not the entire ship? Why not the other Vose in the bar? What was unique about them?" Jamaica continued.

"The Vose are a small, brown-skinned, black eyed race of superior navigators, pilots, sailors, and magicians," McPeak explained. "As Olsen said they are the universe's traders. They are also masters of magic and the last of the humanoid red meat eaters. Centuries ago they feasted on the slain bodies of their enemies. Many species still fear them today."

"I always thought they were a peaceful species," Jamaica said.

"They are. Still there are those who believe that the desire for red meat and the flesh of other beings is still a narcotic the Vose crave. Some Fourth Levelers, underground city dwellers, still eat red meat, raw. They are reported to be the most savage, cunning and magical of the species. They rarely venture past the Third Level, the Magician's Level, and do not travel the stars because as their Great Leader Teea Thar said, 'they travel in their minds.'"

"McPeak is correct. Physical exertion takes too much work from the games of the mind. When Fourth Levelers move, they appear to move in slow motion," Olsen said.

"Vose live in underground cities heated by solar cells and surrounded by lush, tropical vegetation, wild animals, perfumed air and the imports of six planets. But their true love is space and the feel of the open sky on sailing ships. Vosian space ships are the fastest in the Galaxy. No one has been able to duplicate the speed which the solar cells and sails of *haruko* , you know the Vosian plant used to make space ship sails, gives them," McDonald said.

"Their sailing ships resemble the old, three-masted schooners which traveled earth's oceans during the 14th through 18th Centuries. I've lived with the Vose off and on for four years. Those on the first and second level are excellent traders and navigators. The other levels do not engage in space travel. There are six levels of Vosian life. I don't think they can go to another level, voluntarily. That is unless you are a first or second level dweller. Somehow they have special privileges. You are either born into your level or granted a new higher level by the authorities. I don't know what one would have to do to be granted such a favor. There are references of level changes in the Vosian history books. The only ones who still eat raw red meat are the Fourth Levelers. Their women are said to be the most beautiful in the universe. The Third Levelers are master magicians and conjurers. It is said that a Third Leveler can make anyone believe anything. I wouldn't want to test them. I also don't think that the Third Level had anything to do with the men's deaths," Olsen spoke slowly, his fingertips playing with his hair, as he continued his description.

"They're clever, excellent mind players. They'll fight over their women. They throw the bones; it's a prayer for answers." Olsen volunteered a puzzled look before the others could ask.

"Turnin folks into crystal, I never heard of that, not even in the legends. And if they could, why? The *Calliope* appears to be an ordinary trading vessel. Only Second Levelers have ever served aboard her. There aren't any inter level wars. This is strange. I don't like mysteries. I don't even like reading them." McDonald added.

"You folks are the best in the force. You'll just have to find out what's killing folks. Is it a virus, murder, a new weapon? Sabotage? Are all of us in danger? What's the common link? Are the people of Vos in danger? McPeak said.

"Olsen, you report to the *Calliope* with Fitzsimmons, see what you can find. Maybe your knowledge of the Vose will pick up something the rest of us would miss. Keep me informed. But I don't want to know every time a butterfly sneezes. Both of you tend to give too much information," He added smiling.

"McDonald, you and Daliz go to the *Clea*. We don't have tracers in place yet. Meet with General 0-24-3. He speaks International English and Ern. He wants this thing contained. The *Clea,* being military, well they've been able to keep a lid on the deaths, but not for long. They want answers as much as we do. Their folks have turned to dust, not burned or crystallized like ours, or the Vose. More like aged rapidly. Not much for them to autopsy." Mopping his brow with a large checkered red and white handkerchief, he continued.

"Daliz, find out what you can about the Tapias. It's a pretty closed society considering they're our neighbors, out here. Find out if there's a clan war or tribal dispute that we don't know about. Anything that might shed some light on this. McDonald, you'll have to go in disguise. The Tapias don't allow earth women on their station. Go as a Maposian Mystic, they're accepted everywhere. Jordan, in illusions—it's the government's best department for those who should be undercover. They will give you all you need. As you know, females are of little consequence to the Tapias. They are treated as fourth-class beings with little rights. The women aboard the *Clea* or on any of the Tapia gun ships are the only children of the Tapia military elite. The Tapias are the only society in the galaxy in which men and women are not equal. They never listen to women on matters of policy. Remember your role. Any questions?"

"No questions, Sir." They stood and followed Olsen out of the office.

Shutting the door behind them, McDonald asked, "Is Jamaica coming with us?"

"I don't think so. I don't know what McPeak's going to do with her. I warned her about him. I think I should have warned him about her. Let's go."

"What about me, Sir?" Jamaica stood by the conference table, still holding the flashdiscs in her hand.

"Why aren't I going with Neils? He's my partner."

"You'll come with me. I understand that you were first in your class in interviewing techniques. You also specialize in ballistics and forensics. We might as well get you started right away. The *Galileo's* going to be your home for the next six months, so no time to waste in getting a feel for the place," a preoccupied McPeak replied, while rubbing the grey and black stubble on his chin. *Damn, I've forgotten to shave again*, he thought.

Pushing the intercom, McPeak yelled at a Jeeves 322.

"Find the tracers that just left. Tell them that we'll coordinate our information daily at 0630, 1300 and 1900 hours. Jamaica, come with me," They walked to the main elevator and went to Santana Collins' home.

"We'll retrace each dead person's activities in the order of their deaths, maybe that'll tell us something," McPeak said.

Chapter 7

Captain Kalt and Plas stood in front of the fully awakened crew of 150, they glowed blue then deep purple, finally green. Murmurs ran through the crew, who responded in blues and purples.

"Crew, you need to know the hum... cough... desperate situation that we're in. It has been a solar day since I sent the last distress probe. I have been attempting to reach our sister ships. I have not been successful. Nor have I received a response from either of the artificial moons or the planet, there." She gestured to the large cloudy planet on the horizon and continued.

"The ZIXC is caught in the gravitational orbit of this planet which looms so near us. We are stuck on the far side of an unknown star cluster and no one knows where we are."

More murmurs and sharp yellows filtered through the purple.

"As you know, we are the only ship carrying the serum needed on Geaha."

More sharp purples assaulted her eyes, and then calming greens spread through the crew.

"I am sorry to have alarmed you. I need your collective energies to contact the life forms on the cloudy planet." Willing herself green, she continued.

"I have tried to communicate with the beings on the cloudy planet and to those on the moons which circle her. We are equal distance from the moons. Plas and I have monitored their speech. You, Gorn—" she turned to speak to the ship's medical officer, "you are our best linguist and highest empath. Perhaps if you tried…"

She pushed the *ZIXC's* view screen into place to reveal the interior of the *Clea's* observation tower, in which four pink-clad ensigns scanned the sky, unaware that they were being observed. Two very vocal ensigns spoke in low tones near a large panel board.

"Did you hear about the early shift?" one said to the other.

"We're not to speak about that. I asked Commanding Officer 00-4-69 about what we heard. He would not answer my questions. He replied that the early shift was 'ill'."

"Ill? I know someone in medical who told me that the crew had turned to dust. But when I went to him to confirm our earlier conversation, he'd been sent to the next ship leaving for Tapia. He still had six weeks left on his tour," 0-36-97 replied, his voice filled with worry.

"Six weeks left?"

"Yes, I know that he's being punished for speaking to me. I'm not asking any questions. You shouldn't either. Did you see 00-9-47 score the last goal in last nights Ens game?"

"Ens game? Oh yes, great comeback."

The *ZIXC's* crew listened to the ensigns' comments, spread their fingers in the air in order to feel the sound waves, to absorb the moans, hums and whistles which make up the Tapia language.

"This noise is harsh," Gorn said, his fingertips glowing purple. He listened intently, his palms held up to the sound waves he received from the *Clea*. He shook his head and continued.

"The words hurt my fingers. They are rough. The beings are in panic. I don't know what they fear but there is something wrong. I don't believe that they know we are here or in danger."

"We must ask for guidance. Prepare for the Sixth Sheep", Kalt replied with solemnity. The crew nodded in agreement and shook their sore fingers, which confirmed Gorn's sense of fear.

Again Gorn spoke. "The small beings which inhabit the artificial worlds of this planet are frightened. Frightened beings could be dangerous especially if they are as primitive as these life forms appear to be."

"Are all of them as primitive as this moon?" Kalt asked.

"No, the tones coming from the round white moon are softer, yet frantic. Their main language seems to be the same as that on the cloudy planet, soft, quiet, breathy. Listen closely." With hands outstretched, the crew remained very calm and still, and listened to each sound wave.

"The tones were too faint," said one sharp yellow Geahan.

"I can't hear them," replied another.

"Calm yourself. Struggle to hear," Gorn said.

Even my fingers are not sensitive enough to read the sounds, he thought, while attempting to calm others.

"There is a third artificial world, perhaps..." Kalt asserted, his words momentarily floating above him.

Galt moved in front of the viewer and placed his fingertips close to the inner shield.

"This language is simple," he said. "I can master it in a few hours. Perhaps I can try after the Sixth Sheep." The soft hairs surrounding his mouth glowed a calming dark green, then the rest of his body lightened to pale green. The crew sensed his lack of concern and also relaxed.

Floating away from the crew, Kalt and Gorn went to her private chambers.

"Gorn, I know that you are the most intelligent crew member with me. I am deeply honored. Your skills as a linguist are well documented. However..."

"However, my leaps in logic have been a source of concern on Geaha. I've been ridiculed as a dreamer and a philosopher," he muttered.

"Gorn, you're a good friend," Kalt began.

"I know why I'm here. I am most grateful that you are giving me an opportunity to prove my theory of sentient life forms beyond the Geahan home planet system. I think the beings on those moons out there prove my theory. I've speculated about cognitive beings on the other side of the galaxy nearly all my life. You're my closest friend. If I'm correct

I want you to share in the glory."

"And if you are wrong. It won't matter because no one on Geaha will learn of our fate."

"Kalt?"

"Yes?"

"Uh... nothing."

I can't tell her, Gorn thought. *I haven't told anyone, not even the High Commissioner, the only other person on Geaha beside Kalt who doesn't believe me to be mad, that I heard sounds from a small battered mechanical object that passed through Geahan space when I was 15. Maybe it is time for Kalt to learn about the object, which crashed in the desert near my home. She would be curious about the two biped figures, one taller than the other, with differing external body parts carved on the object's exterior. I should let her see the battered and pock marked gold 15 x 23 centimeter message attached to the object's side. It shows a sun and planet symbols. The words or sounds are much like the sounds coming from one of the artificial moons. But it can't be from this solar system. The second planet from this sun has artificial moons. Yet, the sounds are familiar. No, it isn't time to say anything.* He floated away from Kalt and stared at the distant crescents.

"I must prepare the crew for the Sixth Sheep. I will await you in the chapel," Kalt said as she left her chambers.

"I will be right there," Gorn replied.

THE SIXTH SHEEP

The circular chapel floor was pale pink silicate with intricate line drawings etched in the salt. A mouth blown pale green glass bowl four feet in circumference and filled to the shallow brim with liquid Mbongo, holy water made from the essence of departed Geahan priests who spent their adult lives on Mbongo, is in the center of the floor. The crew, temporarily opaque, entered the chapel in single file led by the lowest ensign and stepped into the barely visible bubble prints of the person ahead of them.

Forming six concentric circles, called sheep, they framed the glass bowl. Each was clad in a pale pink gauze-like hooded garment that covered their entire body, leaving only their arms bare.

Captain Kalt, the last to enter, took her place closest to the bowl. The crew began to chant the prayer for safety.

A large pink crystal-like globe, a miniature of the Geahan home planet, rose from the liquid Mbongo. Rising with the globe were two small suns and five tiny moons. The duplication was complete.

The crew reached out to each other and placed two of their three fingers on two fingers of the person on each side. The first and second fingers of Kalt's left hand lay submersed in the liquid; resting near her right eye was the right hand of the lowest ensign. The connection was complete.

A collective chant resounded through the *ZIXC*, echoed off the walls, filling the void outside the ship for 50 meters. However, some on the space stations heard the chant.

Aboard the *Galileo* the animals in the rain forest were quiet. Birds stopped singing. They tried to understand a language, which came to them from the walls, the leaves, and the soil in an ancient and almost forgotten idiom. The butterflies strained to hear the words, which were only cell-memories.

"Cough... cough... good! For a moment I thought I'd lost my hearing. Have you ever found it so quiet?" a botanist said, stepping over a fresh circle of mushrooms with care.

"Never... shush... listen."

The botanist's companion, straining to hear the sound, turned to the botanist and replied.

"I think... look... there—that leaf. I did hear it fall. What's going on?"

Her words were lost in the sudden noise, as each bird and animal seemed to be singing, growling, braying or calling all at once at the top of their voices. Putting their hands over their ears the scientists sat beneath a tree for ten minutes until the deafening noise ceased.

Gathering in the checkerboard squares of the main village on the *Bole,* Third Levelers threw animal bones on the white squares. Conjurers sprinkled ground black marble over the dried *Urd* bones. Blue smoke carried green Vosian fireflies to the bottom of the Second Level where they threw themselves at the Second Level shield. Most died.

An elder Third Leveler, her wrinkled brown palm blackened by the marble dust, gathered her massive maroon caftan close to her withered body. Frowning, she studied the flames.

"How can we send word? We cannot break the barrier. It was a time of great mourning. Many souls on the other side are dying. They call for help. We have done our best. Someone or something else would have to send the message forward." Her aged voice cracked as tears formed behind her third eye and drained into her throat.

Pausing during his investigation on Level Two, Olsen sat with several Level Three dwellers detained for their own safety in the Timossi Outpost, and rubbed his fingers across his scar.

"Who are you?" he asked.

"We are of no consequences. We are mostly magicians," said one of them dressed in the iridescent silks of a space traveler as he looked at a spot six inches above Olsen's head, his voice slow, his words dragging.

"Of no consequences? I understand that you are here because someone accidentally insulted some Naresh space travelers. You're to remain here until the Neptunians depart."

"It was a misunderstanding. Nothing to concern tracers,"

the Leveler replied. His two companions, deep in a state of enrapture, had not spoken.

Oh, no, enrapture. What is going on? This is not something that off worlders witness, Olsen thought, and got up to leave the Levelers to their hypnotic trance.

"I must remember to speak to McPeak about this when I call in," Olsen said to himself.

In five minutes the Levelers "awakened" and continued their wait uninterrupted.

###

"Sir, look at this," 00-97-3 said, as he pointed to the small white substance that clung to the main air supply pump on the *Clea.*

"Do you think this may have caused the contamination?" Shouting above the continuing alarms, he waited for a response.

"Humph... inform the ships that personnel are to continue to transport to waiting ships until we know more."

"But sir..."

"Ensign. I believe that I have given you an order."

"Yes sir."

No one aboard the *Clea* heard the Geahan chant.

###

Four of the *ZIXC's* sister ships returned to Geaha and their crews were sent home, most to face death from the plague. The *Moor,* commanded by one of the few male ship captains, Ncha's grandson, Voig, was resupplied and sent in quest of the *ZIXC.*

"Sir, we have cleared the wormhole."

"Good, good. Is there any sign of the *ZIXC?*"

"No, sir."

"Captain, Captain. Please come to shuttle bay ten," an anxious voice echoed through the bridge.

"On my way."

"Hurry, sir."

"What is it?" Voig asked, floating past five crew members who surrounded a Geahan distress beacon.

"It may be from the *ZIXC,* sir."

"How did it get here?"

"From the wormhole, sir."

"The wormhole?"

"Yes, sir—from the wormhole."

"How? Ensign, thank you. You and the others may go. Sese, stay with me."

Voig waited until the crew left the shuttle bay then turned to Sese and asked.

"What do you think? Could this have come from inside the wormhole?"

"Kalt is an excellent captain, even in hibernation, her senses would have alerted her in time to maneuver out of danger. Something else must have happened to her ship," Sese said, floating around the battered and scarred probe.

"It looks like it's been in a few minor collisions with space debris. What this message?" Opening the communication panel Voig and Sese listened to Kalt's message.

"We are not in our solar system. We are in a very crowded solar system with a single third class sun. We are caught in the orbit of a large cloudy planet. Gorn thinks that there are sentient life forms on the planet and on the three artificial moons that orbit her. I do not, at the moment, share his views. The crew is safe. The serum is safe. We will need help to get out of the orbital pull of this planet. We have tried to communicate with the life forms on the planet and moons but have been unsuccessful. The ship has been placed on emergency impulse. This sun's wind trails were caught in a wormhole and brought us with them. I pray that you can duplicate the conditions that brought us to this strange place and rescue us. These illustrations may help identify where we are. Plas has helped draw the coordinates of the alien sun in relationship to the cloudy planet, artificial and natural moons, and star formations, some of which looked like pictures."

"These are the strangest drawings I've ever seen, yet..."

"Sir?"

"Sese, this looks familiar. Let's take these to my cabin. Perhaps my papyrus library can help. Do you remember the legend of the *Pinnae Geahans?*"

"Yes, sir. It is an ancient legend which is much beloved on my side of Geaha. It is said that the *Pinnae* went to live on the far side of the Ibso wormhole."

"Yes, they were members of the Ayle clan, and said to be the most advanced Geahan clan. They were the first to fly and to explore the heavens beyond Geaha," he replied, as he entered his cabin, followed by Sese. Pushing scrolls on the history of the Geahan peoples aside, on the first four shelves to his right, he looked among the large collection of his personal library.

"Sese, somewhere in here," pointing to some of the yellow scrolls, "is the answer on how to find the *ZIXC.*"

Chapter 8

Reviewing the morning's work, Jamaica put the last of the computer discs on the conference table in McPeak's office.

"I've interviewed all the neighbors, friends and relatives of the six burn victims. I have a few hours before I'll finish interviewing the others," she said to McPeak, who barely looked in her direction and replied with a noncommittal grunt.

"None of us are getting anywhere. None of the others have any new leads, or any new information. When is McDonald's death dirge scheduled?"

"What?"

"You haven't heard a thing I've said. I asked when is McDonald participating in the death dirge."

"Nineteen hundred hours in the main coliseum on the *Clea*. Several *Rista* Mystics are helping with the blessing of the soil and she's been invited to participate," McPeak replied, intently studying a statistical disc.

"McDonald said that the *Clea's* High Command are being very low-key about the deaths," Jamaica continued, in an attempt to make conversation.

Putting the flashdisc down, McPeak looked over to where Jamaica was working and said, "Hum... yes. It may be very difficult to get more information from the *Clea*. Outpost personnel say that the official word is that there had been a breach of security on the observation tower and an unnamed assailant executed all those involved. I guess the soldiers could accept a 'breach of security' as an explanation of the strange comings and goings of doctors, high ranking officers, and tracers better than some invisible virus."

Jamaica stood to outline the accumulated information on an incident board and said, "This is what we know at the moment."

On the *Bole:* 17 Vose crystallized... wrapped in white silk; *Yona* rum, also crystallized. Not only has the rum in the trader's glasses but also that in the bottles on all the bar shelved on Vos and the *Bole,* all crystallized. No other rums or other liquor effected.

"What is the common element? Rum, traders, and white silk. Hardly the makings of murder or sabotage."

"Hum... what did Neils send us from the *Clea?*" McPeak asked.

Clearing a space beside the *Bole* information, Jamaica began to write.

Eight crew members on the *Clea* and one member of the war vessel, *Yrr,* have died. Their bodies turned to dust. Four of the *Clea* crew was in the observation tower and three in the computer room. The *Yrr* was moored at pier 111 when the crew member died. Let's see, what else do we have. Two Tapias were female. None of the eight were from the same clan or village. The only common element that we've been told is that all were out of uniform when the dust-filled clothing was found. Why the Tapias reported something as trivial as that we have to guess. I haven't found anything in common with those on the *Bole.*"

"The military. Being out of uniform could have meant that they were spying," McPeak replied, rubbing his eyes with his index finger and thumb. He got up with a loud grunt and poured himself a cup of coffee.

"Make a column for those here on the *Galileo.*"

"Yes, sir."

Stepping back a few minutes later, they read what Jamaica had written.

Nine confirmed injured. Six dead. The common elements: Hawkins was drinking or had recently drunk *Yona* rum before being burned to death. Rum crystals were found fused to the bottom of his boat. Something to do with the rum.

"Sir, I checked the supply. Hawkins got his from the Earth ship *Magellan* two weeks ago. The rum the traders in Rick's Café drank was new from Mapu. The Vosian rum supply was from an old batch. Perhaps blood type might have something to do with why Earthers were burned and Vose crystallized."

"Did someone say that Mark Kim was out of uniform when he was burned? Let me see that chart," McPeak asked, as he took the copy of the hospital report from Jamaica.

"Yes, here it is. He was wearing white overalls instead of the regulation pink. The Tapias were also out of uniform. Humm, what is the material of Harris' uniform?"

"Cotton."

"And the Tapias?"

"They use a synthetic based mea material. Cotton and mea do not have any of the same molecules. Besides, Collins and Harris weren't wearing uniforms or cotton when found. Collins was wearing a pale antique dressing gown and Harris light silk pajamas. The Buckleys were nude. The white bed coverings were made of muslin. Nothing in common with the others. In fact none of the Earthers have anything in common with each other. Darrow was alone, tending his roses. He was wearing a green suit and Ms. O'Brien was eating chicken soup. There must be something right in front of our noses that we can't see because it's so obvious. I know you've discarded the idea that color might..." Jamaica pondered, and peered at the outlines on the make shift board.

"We've already decided that color, what a crazy idea, is not the problem," McPeak replied, in dismissal of Jamaica's theory while it was still being formed.

"Hawkins always carried rum with him when he camped. He purchased four liters of *Yona* rum just before he entered the river at encampment 14. The Vose were drinking *Yona* rum. There's a connection," Jamaica said softly, for the moment bowing to her supervisor's statement.

"Uh hum," McPeak muttered mostly to himself.

"There wasn't any rum in his flask when he was found,"

McPeak replied. He returned to his battered chair, which squealed in protest to his bulk. He rested his hands on his stomach and looked out the window. Not saying anything for a few minutes, Jamaica sat in silence to allow the puzzle to work its way through his mind.

"There were tiny crystal beads in the bottom of Hawkin's flask, which are being analyzed to determine if they're crystallized rum," Jamaica said.

"Oh no, the alarms. Not again," she said and scrambled for safety as the *Galileo's* main shutters sealed the exterior windows. She and McPeak raced to the main observation port to see if they could discern the source of the problem.

"Medic, medic," a young woman cried. Jamaica wrapped her assistant in cy bandages.

"Someone will be here soon. Take it easy. He'll be okay."

"What are the damages?" McPeak asked a passing tracer.

"Nine more people are burned, four seriously, the others have died. I don't have any other information, sir."

"Thank you. Go about your duties," a solemn McPeak replied. "Jamaica, come with me to a security halovision. We need to find out what's happening on the *Clea* and the *Bole*."

"Neils, McDonald, what's happening? Where you are?" McPeak questioned, as he studied the anxious faces of his people.

"The entire crew on the *Clea's* observation deck has died. We were there when they died."

"Oh, no," Jamaica cried.

"Fortunately neither of us were harmed, nor was the station commander. It all happened in a second. We—no one— had time to react. It was as if lightning had struck. The crew never made a sound."

Neils' words ran together like someone in a hurry to get to something positive.

"Keep me informed. I'm going to check in with Olsen and uh... uh..."

"Fitzsimmons, sir..." Jamaica replied.

"Ah yes, Fitzsimmons." McPeak broke the connection and

contacted Olsen.

"No new casualties from the latest 'false alarm.' No one else's been crystallized during any of the latest alarm problems," Olsen continued. "Nerves are raw and people are frightened. Even some of the old timers are speaking of the safety of their home planet. The collision alarms have sounded only five times previously in the thirty years since the Joint Space Administration deployed the three space stations. The previous alarms warned of erratic meteors, and in 2183, the comet Sorenson came within 10,000 kilometers of the *Bole* before burning up in the sun's atmosphere. Everyone's on alert."

"Same here. The crew is looking at every nut and bolt of the security system. We're telling ships to sail to Mbongo or Vos rather than become 'contaminated' by whatever is affecting our systems," Jamaica said.

"Captain, there is something wrong. I felt an intense surge of panic immediately following the last of our probes," Gorn said with hesitation.

"Whatever has panicked the creatures on those moons, our harmless probe was not the cause. It sends a coded distress message, as well as a message of friendship in all known Heru languages and dialects. You looked at it. It was a common probe. One that absorbs energy through the light spectrum. It uses the major natural propellant on Geaha. Our probe couldn't possibly harm any living thing," Kalt replied. She eased herself closer to the viewing port near Gorn.

"At least none that we have encountered before. I cannot help ignore that my first feeling was one of panic. There is something, anguish and great sorrow among the beings on two of the moons. It happened near the time that our search probe passed through the moons. The energy that it gathered from the light matter should not be harmful to any of the life forms. It is very confusing."

"Our probe is harmless. It is just a coincidence," Kalt

replied, and drifted from the room where Gorn continued to listen.

Chapter 9

"One of the first things you must learn as a tracer is to know your own limits. You've pushed yourself too far. Go home, get some rest. I want you alert and ready to work hard later on," McPeak said in a firm, fatherly voice.

"I know you won't take your own advice. You need rest also. You're going to be working just as hard as I," Jamaica replied and walked out of his office toward the habitat elevators.

"I will get some rest. I'm barely existing on adrenalin and caffeine," she said to herself. She exited the elevator and walked slowly to the door to her small one-bedroom apartment. Opening the door and stepping over clothing she'd carelessly dropped on the floor, she picked up those thrown over furniture and searched for something clean to replace the clothes she'd worn for the past twenty-four hours.

"I must have something clean," she said in an attempt to keep herself awake. The halovision flashed, indicating stored messages.

"Hi, Honey, your father and I hope all is well. We haven't heard from you, which is a sign that you're probably working too hard. Can you tell us anything about the rumors we're hearing about people being burned? Take care of yourself. Call us. I'll be home for the next two months. Kofi and I need to conduct some old fashioned research."

"Hi Jamaica, remember your old dad? We could get together for a chess match. Or just to talk. You left rather abruptly. We miss you." Xi Sung's image faded as the halomessage ended.

"Hi Jamaica, remember me? Hannah—Neil's wife. Thought you might like some home cooking. I know how Neils gets when he's on a case forgetting to eat or call or... if you have time call. I'd love to have you over tonight. Just spaghetti, little wine. What d'you think? Call me."

Smiling at Hannah's fading image, Jamaica punched in her halovision number.

"Hannah—I just got in. Don't look around, the apartment's a mess. I'd love to join you for dinner. Can I bring anything?"

"No, just yourself. It'll be nice to have some company. Eight o'clock okay?"

"Eight's fine. It'll get me time for a short nap." Jamaica broke the connection and walked into the small kitchen.

What about food? Do I have any food? she wondered as she stood in front of the tiny refrigerator, devoid of anything edible. *I guess I forgot to stock the fridge. Doesn't matter, I'm eating at Hannah's. I need a shower, that's what I need, and some tea. But first I need some sleep. Wine—where'd I put the wine?*

Rummaging through a few half empty boxes, she retrieved a bottle of Oak Park Chardonnay from under a stack of clean towels.

"Okay Jamaica, you have your house warming gift. Now you need some sleep." Pushing relatively clean clothes off the bed, she lay down and fell asleep immediately.

Six hours later, she woke to the halovision tone.

"Hi Jamaica, hope you are still speaking to me. I know I said some pretty rotten things before you left. I'm really sorry. I miss you. Bet you're having fun. Call me. Andrew."

His image faded before Jamaica awakened enough to answer. Walking over to the storage center, she replayed the message and smiled. Yawning and stretching to wake herself, she pulled off her dirty clothes and took a long hot bath.

A Mickey Mouse wind-up clock on the back of the toilet announced 5:30.

"Good, I have time to buy food—something other than nutrition bars," she said with a loud yawn and lay back into the soapy hot water. Fifteen minutes later, dressed in a clean sweat suit, she began to unpack in earnest.

She placed tracer clothing in the closet and picked up rumpled and dirty clothing for cleaning. Adjusting the volume on her audiotape to a piercing loudness, she played her favorite "let's clean" music, Martinez Jones's *Third Movement in G minor*. Moving old-fashioned three-dimensional books to a shelf behind the sofa, she took the stack of tracer flashdiscs from the living room sofa where she'd dropped them on the small kitchen table when she entered.

Tapping the flashdiscs with her right index finger, she thought, *there's a vital clue hidden somewhere in these and I'm determined to find it and solve these burn deaths.* The music, which she always played loud enough to almost harm her eardrums, echoed off the walls as she moved from room to room putting things away, hanging pictures, and arranging her jade pieces.

"I heard about your green grocer when I was stationed on the Earth's moon." Jamaica said to Noah Smith, owner of Smith's Groceries, situated on the 200th floor.

"Did you now? From Earth's moon."

"Yep, you're supposed to have the best California kiwi and Saari alo in the galaxy."

"I have a reputation to uphold. My family's been green grocers on Earth for centuries. I've been on the *Galileo* for four years," he replied while wrapping four tiny fuzzy brown kiwis into her shopping net.

"Reputation, huh? Your ancestors would be very proud of your 'green' thumb."

"Thanks for the compliment. Anything else?"

"Yes, I'll have four baskets of strawberries and two bunches of carrots. At least I'll have fresh fruit and veggies for snacks when I return to the office."

"Ah yes, fruits and vegetables. Something of substance for the body and soul."

"Yep, something besides coffee and tea. I've been asking too much of caffeine."

"Hi, come in. Nice to see you again. I've also invited Carl Starr, from the zoo, to join us for dinner," Hannah said as she took the bottle of wine from Jamaica and kissed her cheek.

"I'll take your coat. The Jeeves is in the kitchen with Carl, fixing the salad," Hannah continued as Jamaica entered the spacious apartment.

"Wow, I really like the way you've decorated your place. Sorta like a Bedouin market place," Jamaica remarked as she looked around the plush, carpeted living room, which was filled with large colorful throw pillows, footstools and low sofas.

"I expect to see a camel poking its head in from the door any second."

"In place of camels, there's No Pi L, my parrot."

"Oh yes! Neils told me a lot about him. I don't have any pets. What's that strange song he's repeating? It really intrigues me," Jamaica asked, making herself comfortable in a large paisley sofa.

"Hi, you must be Jamaica," said a tall, thin young man who entered the living room, a steaming spoon of spaghetti sauce in his outreached hand.

"Taste?"

"Tastes wonderful."

"Thanks, I wish I could make half-way decent spaghetti sauce. Mine's always too watery. Hannah's here is perfect," he said as he sipped the last drops of sauce and licked the spoon.

"I haven't met any tracers other than Neils. Have you been on the *Galileo* for a long time?" Carl asked, chewing on his thumb knuckle.

"I've just arrived. Actually, three days ago. I've been very busy on a complicated case. Hannah, I'm working on Heather O'Brien's death. Did you know her?"

Hannah shook her head. Jamaica turned back to Carl and

continued.

"I'm really glad that Hannah asked me over. I need a break. My brain's gone to mush. I need to meet people other than tracers, victims or relatives for a while. Tonight, I just need to relax. So Carl, I'm very pleased to meet you also."

"I haven't eaten a home cooked meal in over six months. I don't own a Jeeves, so I eat most of my meals at fast food outlets," Carl replied.

"You live alone?"

"Yep, I been divorced for three years. Great woman, Sara, but I lived for the zoo and with my voluntary vet's practice in the evenings. I left her alone too much. She's remarried. I really miss her." Carl continued to settle in a comfortable overstuffed chair in front of the fireplace, next to the sofa on which Jamaica sat.

"I'll join you two in a minute," Hannah said, walking into the kitchen. "I need to stir the sauce and put on the pasta."

"Do you want any help?" Jamaica called after her.

"No, you two just relax. I'll be right back," Hannah replied. "Besides, Neils told me that you burned water. Neils does most of the cooking when he's home, so I can identify with you. Our Jeeves 322's already made the salad and set the table. Relax."

Over dinner and wine, the three engaged in small talk about Earth for the next hour.

"Where you from?" Carl asked Jamaica.

"Sacramento, California, Old Earth. And you?"

"New America on the moon. You, Hannah?"

"Nebraska, Old Earth."

All three spoke of their strong family ties and the adventure of deep space travel, the renovations of the tenth floor of the *Galileo* and the latest Earth moon colonies. No Pi L remained on his perch in the corner of the living room, on occasion talking softly to no one.

"I thought I was familiar with most inner planet languages. I don't understand No Pi L's language. What is he saying?" Jamaica asked as she sipped her second glass of wine and took another helping of spaghetti.

"I don't know. He began talking to himself just after we arrived. We'd been here for three months, two years ago. He didn't chat at all then. Now it seems as if he's trying to memorize something. Of course he's older now and still learning. I'm still amazed at all he has learned so far."

"Parrots are remarkable birds. I'm always charmed when I'm around one," Carl replied.

After dinner, they returned to the living room. While the Jeeves 322 cleaned up, Hannah and her guests continued their small talk.

"I'm really relaxed. I better not have any more wine. Perhaps some coffee before I go home. I hadn't realized how tense and tired I've been," Jamaica said.

"You've chosen my favorite piece," Jamaica said, turning toward the audio disc's gentle flute and guitar music.

"Martinez Jones is one of my favorite composers also," Hannah said.

"Carl, I'm learning more about zoos than I thought possible," Jamaica said. "How did you two meet?" Jamaica asked Hannah and handed a fresh wine glass to Carl.

"We met in Bagaces, Costa Rica, on Earth. We were both grad students," they said in unison. Both laughed, Carl continued.

"I went on to veterinary school and became a veterinarian, while Hannah went on to receive her doctorate in avian linguistics. Now here we both are on the *Galileo*."

"Carl came by to see if I had ever..."

"Help!" A loud call from No Pi L interrupted Hannah's sentence. Flying from his perch to Hannah on the sofa, he continued his cry.

"Help. Help us. We're caught. Help."

Carl and Jamaica jumped up and rushed to the parrot's aid.

"He appears to be in distress. Look how he keeps flexing his pupils, raising his crest and fanning out his tail feathers."

Carl examined the small bird.

"Help, help us. We're caught. Help!" Flying to the exterior

window, No Pi L pecked at the glass.

"Help."

"He doesn't seem injured," Hannah said. "He seems a little calmer."

"What are those words? He's begun repeating the same words. Do you think he hears something or someone we can't?" Jamaica asked.

"I have no idea. I've never heard him say anything like this before," Hannah replied. She gulped her wine, poured more and sipped the second glass. She smoothed No Pi L's feathers and sat down next to Carl on the sofa.

"First your flamingos, and now No Pi L. What's happening to the birds?" she whispered.

"What's this about flamingos?" Jamaica asked.

"I came over to see if Hannah had ever heard of a disease that turned flamingos' feathers white. Whatever it is, it's killed all the flamingos on the *Galileo*. It hasn't affected the birds on Earth. My flamingos came from three different countries, yet they all caught the disease. It must be something here on the station." Carl looked over to No Pi L.

"He looks okay. It's like he's hearing something we can't hear," Carl shook his head and continued. "Now even I'm turning him into a dog. I doubt No Pi L can hear anything the three of us can't."

"I was thinking the same thing." Hannah stroked the bird and spoke to him in a calming voice.

Pausing, Carl looked over at Jamaica. "Are you okay?" he asked a shaken Jamaica.

Managing a nod, she took a sip of wine and sat down on the chair.

"How," she coughed as her voice caught, "how did the flamingos die?"

"It was heat stroke. Strangest thing, they sort of cooked internally. I've never seen anything like it," Carl replied.

"Neither have I. We've looked through all the medical journals we have on the *Galileo*. I've placed a call to the Avian Labs at the University of California, Davis, for any additional help or support," Hannah added.

"Why are you so concerned about the flamingos? I thought Neils said you didn't have any pets."

"I don't have pets. But I'm wondering if the flamingos' disease might have something to do with my cases. Some *Galileons*—Heather O'Brien, for one—have died under mysterious circumstances, much like your birds. And No Pi L's language strikes a chord. Something from my rookie year. I wish I could remember it. A myth or fable from the Saari. Yet he was speaking English. Besides, the nonsense words aren't from Saar. His words are more lyrical. Did you autopsy the flamingos?"

"Yes. But we didn't find anything. You're welcome to come to the zoo's hospital tomorrow and look at what we have. None of the zoo's workers have become ill or died, so I don't know how your people could have been infected," Carl replied as he placed another log on the fire and Hannah refilled their wine glasses.

"I don't know either. It's a shot in the dark. Maybe there's a connection. I've been unable to find a connection between the humans, much less with flamingos. No Pi L seems calm now. Whatever was bothering him must have gone away," Jamaica said. She looked over at the parrot that appeared to be sleeping.

"Speaking of going away, I really must leave. I have an early morning meeting tomorrow. Carl, I will take you up on the visit to the hospital, is 10:30 okay?"

"Okay. It's been a wonderful evening. I look forward to tomorrow. Hannah, I must go also. Thanks for the great dinner and wine. Tell Neils that I owe you two a good dinner when he returns."

Hannah walked Jamaica and Carl to the door and said, "Carl, I believe that I'll come to the hospital tomorrow, also. If Jamaica's correct and there is any correlation between your birds and what happened to Heather, then I want to know what it is. I didn't know her but she worked in the Amazon Laboratory. See you then."

Handing Carl the briefing flashdisc they discussed earlier, she hugged him goodbye.

"Jamaica, thanks for the wine. I'd forgotten how much I miss California wine. See you tomorrow."

They hugged and parted.

"Well, No Pi L, what is this strange song you've been repeating? And who have you been listening to?" Hannah said. She stroked her pet and turned off the lights. Sitting by the fire, she and No Pi L listened to the music.

Aboard the *ZIXC*, Gorn fought sleep, tiring from his attempts at communication. "I believe that I've made contact with a sentient being on one of the artificial moons. If I'm correct, perhaps it understands and help will come."

Aboard the *Clea,* trouble was brewing. When McDonald sensed that the Tapias were preparing for battle, he decided to eavesdrop on conversations.

"Someone on the other space stations is sabotaging our station," more than one Tapia said to another when they thought they were alone.

"I have to find Neils and warn him of my feelings. Maybe he's heard or seen something that will confirm my suspicions," said McDonald.

Chapter 10

Looking around the normally busy depot where he'd arranged to meet McDonald, Neils glanced at his watch. *She's late. I wonder what's wrong. She's almost never late,* he thought. Everyone else seemed to be in a hurry yet tried to appear casual.

"Something's going on," he said to himself while masking his speech from any Tapias who might be near. He continued to watch busy Tapias as they moved cargo sealed in military tarp to awaiting ships.

The space portal, usually a source of space station gossip, was unnaturally quiet. Sitting near the lounge door of Space Portal 23, Neils nursed a cup of *Galileon* coffee, the only coffee he could drink black and without sugar.

McDonald was rarely late, she seemed to have a built-in time mechanism which helped her to arrive early for most meetings. She was so punctual that other Tracers and Timossi personnel set their time pieces by her arrivals and departures rather than the official clocks. She was a half hour late. Too early to panic, but Neils was getting restless.

Attempting to look as much like a Tapia as possible, Neils was wearing a tight-fitting helmet and glasses. Sitting with his back to the loading pod so the workers wouldn't notice him too much, he kept them under observation. His blond ponytail could easily be mistaken for the blond queues of the valley Tapias. Those on the *Clea* wore their queues very long—nearly to their waist. It was a badge of honor worn to indicate that they serve or had recently served on the *Clea*. Resisting the urge to look at his watch for the fourth time in five minutes, Neils looked up to see McDonald's confident figure approaching from the loading side of the portal.

"I was beginning to worry. Your time clock must be off here on the *Clea*," he whispered as soon as she sat down.

She flashed a conspiratorial smile, showing even white teeth, surrounded by full lips, painted dark red. She touched his hand in a Mystic greeting that acknowledged the enjoyment she felt in her role. She waited until the bar keeper took her order, for Watney's, before replying.

"I've been with a *Rista* delegation that just completed a blessing of a supply ship headed toward Er."

The bar keeper placed the Watney's in front of her.

"Thanks," she said, turning to Neils, who warmed his hands on a refilled cup of coffee.

"There's a build up of Tapia ships on the far side of Cassista. It looks like they are headed this way."

"This way, to the *Clea?*"

"Yes. The *Ristas* have heard that Tusquets, the political leader of the Tapia, has a meeting with 0-24-3 on Er in a week. The Tapias believe that the Vose and we Earthers are trying to prevent them from remaining on the *Clea*." Neils approached her, his mouth open to interrupt with a question, which she raised her hand to prevent. She continued.

"Even though the *Bole* and *Galileo* alarms sounded at the same time as the *Clea's* and people died on the other space stations, the Tapias suspect a conspiracy. You know, they're suspicious of their own shadows. Now this—with the alarms going off and not finding anything. Well, it just adds to their paranoia."

Waving to the deserted portal area, she continued her briefing.

"Tapias just don't turn to dust immediately. There has to be a cause. The air supply is suspect; contaminants were found. The air modules have been replaced and the computers up dated. They suspect the food, clothing, each other, but especially us." Draining her Watney's, she ordered another.

"What you've said makes sense. I've been sitting here for

two and half hours, and the portal is unusually busy, in an unhurried way. I think we should alert McPeak." Looking at his watch, Neils continued, "We're due to call McPeak in an hour."

McDonald turned her head to one side as if listening to someone on the other side of Neils. She did not immediately acknowledge his words.

"What is it? Do you hear something?" Neils asked, swallowing the last of the now very cold coffee.

"I've been having the weirdest feelings ever since I arrived here. Like someone's whispering in my ear but at a level too faint for me to hear. I think that I have to get used to the Tapias' thought waves. They're so erratic and harsh that I tune them out a lot. This other sound is different," she said as her gaze met Neils' puzzled expression.

"Perhaps your special abilities are picking up whatever the Tapias are up to," he replied. She shook her head and said nothing.

"McDonald, you know that you usually down played your empathic sympathies."

"I just want to fit in as a regular tracer, and not one who feels vibrations. But I know that I'd probably still be in the officer's pool if it had not been for my extra-sensory skills. I vacillate between being proud of my skills and wishing to hide them. Today, I want to hide them."

"Believe me—I do understand," Neils replied as they continued to observe the comings and goings of the remaining *Clea* workers for the next half hour.

"I'll leave first. The *Rista* compound is less than five minutes from the outpost. I can make the next call without arousing any suspicions," McDonald said and finished her third Watney's and walked out of the bar.

Neils found an isolated halovision shelter and called Hannah. She wasn't home so he left a message. He called the lab and her assistant told him that she was working at the zoo's hospital, something to do with flamingo deaths. She'd been there most of the day.

Neils headed toward the Timossi Outpost and investigated

the information McDonald had just given him regarding the build up of ships near Cassista while he waited for McPeak's call.

Carl, Hannah and Jamaica arrived at the zoo hospital at 10:30 and worked through lunch and dinner, searching for anything that would give them a clue to the deaths aboard the *Galileo*. Near midnight, Jamaica missed the last call-in from Neils and McDonald. She rubbed her red, hurt eyes and stretched her stiff back.

Between yawns, she said, "I don't know any more about what or how the flamingos were killed than when I first arrived here nearly 11 hours ago. I know even less about any possible connection between the bird's deaths and the humans."

The graveyard shift arrived, and with them the aroma of fresh coffee, donuts and fruit.

"Good, I'm glad someone brought food. I'm starving. Hannah, your dinner seems a lifetime ago," Jamaica remarked, accepting the offer of a lab tech, a young man about her age—of fresh strawberries and cream cheese, along with an herbal tea blend, grown in the Galilean Rain Forest.

"Thanks! These strawberries remind me of the baskets I purchased yesterday. Hope I get home before they spoil."

Jamaica rubbed her tired eyes, returning, somewhat refreshed, to the microscope that held a slide containing flamingo cells. Hannah and Carl spoke in the scientific shorthand of familial workers and continued their experiments with flamingo blood samples. Frustration hovered over their work like a shroud.

"The cells, blood, tissue and body parts all indicated that the birds died as a result of tremendous internal body temperature," Hannah said while setting a slide to the side of her microscope.

"The birds are of both sexes, various ages, come from different countries on Earth, and probably did not have a common ancestor. We've checked DNA and cells without finding any defective quotient," Carl replied to anyone who'd listen.

"This is insane. All these records and samples only confirm what we already know. The flamingos were alive and healthy one minute, then dead next from heat stroke, or something very much like heat stroke. The other birds—canaries, crows, parrots and even the ostriches were unharmed," Jamaica said.

She took a flashdisc from the lab's library. Always curious, she was learning something new about birds. Was she on a wild goose chase? When she uttered those words an hour or so earlier the entire lab staff had laughed. It did ease the tension but didn't answer her question. Could the study of bird innards somehow lead her to the reason for the human deaths as well? It had worked once for ancient Diviners of Earth's past.

Leaving the laboratory at 4:30 a.m. Jamaica went home to take a nap.

"I have to meet McPeak at his office at 7:00 a.m." She left Carl and Hannah still working.

Safely in her bed, Jamaica dreamed something about white things—clouds, ice cream, cotton balls, and teeth. Her mind was filled to overflowing with color, yet it echoed of absences of color. She awoke, as tired and as confused as when she'd gone to bed.

"I spent all day looking at bird parts and cells, and reading material about birds. And I learned a great deal about birds, but nothing about the human or avian deaths," she said the next morning at the beginning of a meeting that lasted less than an hour. Almost feeling as grumpy as she, McPeak said little.

"I'll have some breakfast, then go see Mrs. Darrow."

"Um huh."

She left his office and walked down the ring to a coffee shop, where she had a breakfast of bagels and cream cheese before leaving for Mrs. Darrow's house. She reread the investigative reports over breakfast. The dream returned to her consciousness. She was still concentrating on the color white, or to be more specific, the lack of color. Another common thread was the color pink. She was wearing a dark pink tracer suit today, herself, which was a common color. Jamaica went to a halovision port and called Mariah.

"Hi, Mariah, this is Jamaica."

"No kidding. I thought someone had taken over your body." Mariah peered over stacks of three-dimensional books on a desk as cluttered as the one Jamaica used in McPeak's office. "How are you?"

"Fine, there was something that Serene..." Looking up from her computer screen, Jamaica rifled through a stack of flashdiscs.

"Yes, Serene—the bartender, said about the silk being pink. Did you check further into that?"

"No, the silk is white. I have some, um... a bolt, uh, here in the office." Mariah moved some documents, flashdiscs, and files from in front of her then looked around. Some files fell to the floor, joining a growing pile of debris near her desk.

"I can't find the silk. Pieces are being tested for microbes. The rest is in the property room in the sub-basement," she replied, exhaling a puff of smoke.

"I only smoke when stressed or relaxed," Mariah commented, accompanied by a deep laugh and coughing as the smoke entered her lungs.

Jamaica laughed with her.

"Could you check with a reliable source," she said, "or the traders' log to confirm whether they purchased pink or white silk? I have a theory, but I don't want to alarm anyone until I check out some more things here on the *Galileo*. Oh, and Mariah—" She turned for a moment from the halovision so that her back was temporarily toward Mariah. "Don't wear anything pink for a while," Jamaica continued, "not even underclothes. I'm going to wear blue, my favorite color, until this mystery is solved. I know what I'm saying sounds crazy, and I can't prove anything, yet. I just may be carted off to Napa."

"Where?" Mariah asked.

"It's an old American village, not far from Sacramento, known for its wine. It's also known for its mental institutions. It's an inside California joke."

"Ok, um... I won't wear anything pink for a while. Come to think of it, I don't own anything pink."

"Don't drink any *Yona* Rum, either. If you find out anything, we can discuss it with the whole group at the next call in."

"No Rum? Okay. There's still Samuel Adams. I don't know how you drink only coffee and tea. This job's got me so I know all the best brands of rum, beer, and wine in the universe. But I'll check things out here. Pink, huh, I've been concentrating on a virus or something the traders may have caught or brought back with them. My curiosity is up. Keep me informed."

"It still may be a virus. I've spent the past day looking at bird's—flamingos to be specific—cells. The *Galileo's* zoo's vet thinks the birds died from a virus. We'll see. Where's Olsen?"

"Back on the *Calliope*. He wanted to check out some information some of his sources had uncovered. He thinks it may be black market or pirate stuff. Not anything that will help with the investigation. He'll be back tonight sometime. I'll have him check the log and personnel again before he returns here." They broke the connection.

Jamaica returned to her apartment, put all the white and/or pink things away then redressed and went to visit Mrs. Darrow.

"Mrs. Darrow, remember me, I'm Jamaica Wong. I came to see you a couple of days ago, right after your husband's death."

"Yes, yes, of course, you're the tracer," Mrs. Darrow replied. She wore a smile that didn't quite reach her eyes.

"I finally got rid of all the support people who'd come to check on me since Joplin's death. I need some time alone for a while but I can spare a few minutes for you. I was preparing to send his body... ashes really, back to Earth. Joplin had specified that he wanted his ashes scattered over the Atlantic Ocean. It was spelled out in his will."

Mrs. Darrow continued speaking in a calm voice, but Jamaica noticed her hands shaking as she played with a small handkerchief embroidered with tiny blue flowers.

"Come in. Come in... care for some tea? I've just made a fresh pot," Mrs. Darrow said. She moved aside to allow Jamaica to enter the apartment.

"Don't mind if I do. I won't be very long. There's just a few questions I need to ask you."

A few minutes later, seated in the Darrow's spacious, but cluttered, living room while Mrs. Darrow poured cinnamon spiced tea from an old, heavy, silver teapot, Jamaica opened her transcriber.

"Honey?" Mrs. Darrow asked, adding a generous heaping of honey to her own bone china cup.

"No, thanks, I've never been able to drink tea with anything in it," Jamaica replied. They drank their tea in silence for a short while. Mrs. Darrow's eyes filled with tears but they did not flow onto her face. Blowing her nose self-consciously, she looked over at Jamaica.

"Joplin and I were married for nearly 53 years," Mrs. Darrow began. "We were used to each other. Basically I think we took each other for granted. I always expected him to be here, tending to his roses. I thought that we might..."

Pausing again she blew her nose then continued.

"I thought that we might go together, you know, in a space accident. We've traveled to the inner planets a lot since Joplin retired. I really miss him. Our youngest daughter wants me to come to New America, the moon's colony, to be near her. I don't know... maybe I'll stay here for awhile." She got up and replaced the cool water with some fresh hot water.

After a few minutes Jamaica asked, "Do you know why roses, which are white, were named Wendy's Pink Delight? It seems an odd name for white roses."

Looking puzzled, Mrs. Darrow shook her head.

"I think the shipping package may still be on the balcony. I haven't really done anything except water the older roses since... since he died. I never really paid much attention to them. I'm afraid some of them have died. Roses were Joplin's hobby. I had backgammon. I wish I had paid more attention to his things."

"Don't worry. There wasn't anything you could have done. May I look for the shipping label?" Jamaica asked. She reached over and gave Mrs. Darrow's arm a comforting pat.

"Of course, let's go look for it."

They walked outside to the deck. The rose package was still there, crumbled and torn, lying on the floor near the spot where Joplin Darrow died. Jamaica bent and picked up the package. On prominent display was a color print of a bright white rose and the words *Wendy's Pink Delight*.

"Isn't that strange? The roses were all white. They died, of course. Probably too delicate to survive the transport. And with Joplin dead, I really didn't know what to do with them. I forgot to water them for a day or two. The older ones, the yellows and oranges are still blooming," Mrs. Darrow said in a matter of fact voice.

"Died, yes, I suppose they would be too delicate. Do you still have some of the roses here or have you thrown them all away?" Jamaica asked.

"That's them," she replied and pointed to several shriveled bushes in the corner of the deck.

"I couldn't bear to throw them away yet. They were the last things..." Finally losing the battle with her tears she cried to herself, her sentence unfinished.

Snipping off several pieces from each bush, Jamaica labeled them and put them in her tracer case.

"Thank you so much for seeing me and for the tea. If we find out anything... well, I'll come by personally to let you know. I have others that I must see. I'll let myself out." Maneuvering around the crowded living room, Jamaica quietly let herself out.

Mrs. Darrow remained on the deck for a long time, touched each surviving rose and leaf and continued to weep.

###

"McPeak— Hi, it's me," Jamaica said. "I've just left Mrs. Darrow's home, I might have a lead but I need to speak with the burn victims in the hospital. I'll be there if you need me."

Jamaica left the message for McPeak then took the elevator to the 214th floor of the hospital.

"Jamaica Wong—I'm here to interview Mark Kim, Shirley Van Cale, and Mapuha Smith," Jamaica said as she held out her tracer identification card to an administrator.

"We've been told to expect you. You may have five minutes with each victim. I must insist on having a nurse present in case the patients become distressed."

"Five minutes should be plenty of time. Who do I see first?"

"Mark Kim—he's the most seriously burned, and is recovering slower than anticipated. His body isn't accepting the cy solutions although he's not allergic to the medicine," a nurse named Debisue Leonard said as she opened the door and moved a small wooden chair close to the bed for Jamaica. Mr. Kim was covered in the Juarez material. Cy vapors filtered the air. The room was very soothing.

Jamaica sat close to Mark's head and opened her transcriber as Mark mumbled something incoherent. Debisue gave him a drink of something blue and moved away from the bed. Mark's dark eyes shined brightly. *I wondered if his eyes are bright from pain or just in the contrast of the cy*, Jamaica thought. His eyes and lips were all she could see, the rest of him was covered in cy bandages.

"Mr. Kim—my name's Jamaica Wong. I'm one of the tracers who are trying to find out what happened to you. I only have a few questions." Jamaica felt the pain in his eyes as she turned to face him.

"I'll move the chair closer so you won't have to move. Were you still in uniform when you were burned?"

"Yes." The answer was so weak she missed it.

"What?"

"He said, yes," Nurse Leonard repeated.

Jamaica looked at the nurse and asked, "Mark, was your uniform the regulation pink?"

"Yes." Again, Nurse Leonard spoke.

"You had not changed into a white uniform, had you?"

"No," Mark answered slowly. Jamaica understood him although Nurse Leonard repeated the, 'no."

"Thank you. Rest and get well." Jamaica stood and smiled down at Mark Kim. His eyes were closed. Shaking her head she thought, *what could have caused this?* She walked out of the room as Debisue checked Mark's vitals then followed her out the door.

###

"Shirley Van Cale's room is six down from Mr. Kim's," Debisue said.

When Jamaica opened the door, she saw that Ms. Van Cale looked very much like Mark Kim, covered from head to foot in cy bandages. Her blue eyes looked frightened. Her curly blond hair peeked between cy bandages.

"What were you wearing just before you were burned?"

"Wearing? Not much, I had just finished my bath and grabbed a pink towel that was hanging on the door knob," Ms. Van Cale said, in a voice stronger than Kim's.

"Are you sure the towel was pink?" Jamaica asked.

"Yes, I'm lying here burned very badly. I may never play again. And you're asking me stupid questions about the color of my towel," Ms. Van Cale protested between loud sobs.

She attempted to adjust her position so she could see Jamaica more clearly. Debisue tapped Jamaica on the shoulder and motioned for her to follow her out of the room.

"I'm sorry. But she's taking this whole episode very badly. She's very frightened. I don't think you should ask her any more questions for awhile."

"That's okay. I've gotten the answer I wanted. May I see

Ms. Smith, now?" Jamaica could still hear Ms. Van Cale's sobs from the closed hospital room door.

Mapuha Smith was as mummified as the other two, her bright red hair spiked through the cy bandages like an errant lawn. She looked into Jamaica's cool, green eyes with a direct, steady gaze. *My God!* thought Jamaica, *she's my age or younger. Funny how you draw mental pictures of people based on what they do for a living.* Shuddering at the thought of being confined in a hospital, smothered in bandages, Jamaica put on her clinical, tracer face.

"Hi, my name's Jamaica..."

"After the island on Old Earth?" Mapuha interrupted. She nervously chewed her bottom lip. The cy gauze was discolored around her mouth.

"Yeah, the island. I went there once, as a child," Jamaica answered. *No quick question then out the door, here*, she thought.

"Me, I never went nowhere. Too poor. Then, well... I found these ships... and well... I usta be pretty. Them nurses." Mapuha's eyes darted in Debisue's direction. "They say no scars will show with this new stuff. A girl's gotta have her looks in this business."

"No, there won't be any scars," Jamaica reassured her. "I've seen patients who've used the Juarez materials. I'd love to talk. Perhaps I could come back later, when you're better, okay?"

"Okay. You promise?" Mapuha asked, suddenly looking both very young and very old.

"I promise. Now tell me—what were you wearing when you got burned."

"Wearing? It was a... let me think... of... ah! It was a pale pink Saari walking suit. Yeah, that was it. I remember. I'd just purchased the last one in the ship's store. Pink goes real nice with my red hair. Do ya think them Saari was mad cuz I was wearing one of their things? I mean... what I do and all?" Mapuha asked in a low, soft voice.

"No, I don't think the Saari had anything to do with your accident," Jamaica replied, smiling to herself. *My theory's working out,* she thought and stood to leave.

Placing her small, bandaged hand on Jamaica's arm, Mapuha said, "Ya promised to come see me. Don't forget."

"I won't forget." Jamaica left the hospital and hurried back to McPeak's office.

"Okay, the flamingos, the roses, people's clothing all were originally pink. All had the color removed. But how or by whom?" She spoke for the most part to herself, yet she raised her voice high enough for McPeak to interject should he choose to do so. Jamaica listed her clues.

McPeak remained silent, to all appearances intent on the thick report on his desk, and he appeared to ignore her, except for an occasional "uh huh," as a signal that he was listening. She searched through the flashdiscs scattered on her desk, but still no answers.

"Somehow living things died or suffered badly when they came in contact with something pink. Some of those things, the roses and flamingos were naturally pink. Others, the Tapias, Vose, and some humans died when ingesting or surrounded by something pink," she said, reciting her analysis.

"McPeak, we need to contact Neils and McDonald. I need some information on the Tapias," Jamaica said, She took some of the computer flashdiscs with her as she moved close to McPeak's desk.

###

Olsen returned from the *Calliope* to meet with some of his contacts on Vos. Most were Second Level dwellers and much more experienced in the interworld dealings of other beings than those on the *Bole* or in other sections of Vos.

"What is this we have heard about the strange stories that some of the *Calliope* traders were crystallized on the *Bole?*" asked one of his contacts, who sat in a large, comfortable air-inflated red plastic chair near the external observation windows of

Olsen's apartment. The Vosian settled into the seat and looked around the apartment, decorated in the cold plastic 1950s America look of Olsen's great, great grandparents' world. The yellow sulfuric acid vapors that gave the plastic furniture a soft, warm glow swirled and danced outside the two-foot-thick window.

"I've heard the same thing. It appears to be correct," Olsen replied. He fingered his scar and ran his left hand through his hair.

"Yeah, some story, huh?"

"Yeah, some story," another replied with skepticism.

"You are spending too much time with the Third Levelers. You are beginning to think in riddles," the first Vosian said.

If he, a tracer, believed that Vose could be crystallized in fractions of seconds, well... the Second Leveler thought. Smiling behind his veils, he was too polite to laugh at the Third Level Believers.

"I need your help with my investigation," Olsen said after a moment of awkward silence.

"Has anyone on Vos crystallized like the traders?" he continued.

His visitors shook their heads no, they thought it was best to humor him and attempt to find out what was going on. *If the stories are really true we could all be in danger,* they all thought.

"There is one thing," Adar, the most aggressive of the four Vose, said.

"The Third Levelers have been throwing the bones. They believe that there is a serious rift in the planet's harmony. It is a time of great sorrow. They feel it. It comes from outside."

Adar, a former Third Leveler, still played some of the magic games. *I do not discount my feelings,* he thought to the others.

"Something beyond the Leveler's control is sending messages, we..." Adar stopped in mid-sentence. When his companions looked his way he continued.

"I mean—they—think someone is lost. I can't explain it any better than that."

I thought you were uncomfortable sharing Third Level ideas with outsiders. Even a Convert, one of his companions thought.

"Do you believe this?" Olsen cursed under his breath that he could not thought-transfer like the Vose.

"The world of magic, mystery and chants had no place in the interplanetary world in which I wished to remain," Adar replied.

"The solar winds have been especially strong lately," a Second Leveler said after a few minutes of silence.

"Yes, it has," replied another.

"Have you priced Napoleon brandy? You would think they made it out of spun gold," said another. Moments later, after a few more comments about the weather they left Olsen's apartment.

"Have I been given a clue? What is all this about something or someone connected to the Third Level?" he asked himself as he shut the door behind the last of the Vose.

Chapter 11

Hannah and Jamaica left the lab together and went to their separate apartments. When Hannah returned home, she viewed Neils' message, and left a return message for him.

"Neils, honey. I'll call back near 2 p.m."

She slept for a couple of hours, awakened near 10:00, and decided to bring No Pi L to work with her.

"Little fella, I've only heard your chant here, in the apartment. I need to know if whoever you're talking to can reach you wherever you are on the *Galileo*," she said to the silent bird.

Stepping out of the shower, she heard No Pi L chant, "Help us. We are caught. Help!" She checked the programmed-to-record Jeeves 322 for any chants occurring while she was away but found nothing. No Pi L had been quiet for hours.

She dried off, dressed and return to the lab.

"I wish I knew who was sending you signals," she said with affection while filling the bird's seed bowl.

"You showed remarkable cogitative powers even as a young parrot. You even seemed to sense when things were going badly for Neils or me. It can't be Neils. He's all right. Besides, I've never heard of parrots that could receive messages over long distances. And Neils is over a million miles away." She concluded her breakfast conversation with her pet.

Hannah reached the emergency control for the space station and said, "This is Hannah Daliz. This may sound a little strange, but could you send someone to check the floors above and below mine? Someone may be hurt... No, to tell you the truth, it's my pet. He's repeating 'help me, help me.' I thought he might be hearing someone close by. Thanks, I'll let Neils know." She broke the halovision connection, sat and listened to the soft calls for help coming from the parrot.

"All the people are safe," the tracers reported to McPeak after contacting all the personnel on Hannah's floor, as well as the floors above and below hers.

"You know, sir, we had to go to almost every apartment. Some of these older inhabitants—the pioneers who helped build the space stations or the early scouts to the Sirius region— refused to accept the internal apartment sensory probes, which are the usual features of elderly apartment programming. More than one of them told us that they've endured enough danger for multiple lifetimes and refused the inference that they need help."

"Sir, many of the elderlies live alone and relish the opportunity to do as they 'please after years of government paternalism.' That's a quote, sir," another of the police personnel said.

"Those on the floor above Ms. Daliz are mostly factory workers..."

"Factory workers?" McPeak interrupted.

"Yes, sir, those who make the office equipment that's used to operate the complex machinery," the tall tracer, attempting to shield his impatience with his superior in the presence of Vosian police authorities, replied.

"All are safe and accounted for, and resent the intrusion into their lives as much as the elderlies. Whoever or whatever were sending the signal to Ms. Daliz' pet is not on the *Galileo*," he continued.

"Okay, check the ships in orbit around the *Galileo*. Ask only about the health of the crew," McPeak said.

"I've been informed of the eminent birth of two Maposians on the freighter, *Iowa Maru*. Everything else seems normal. I want you two to follow up."

"Yes, sir," the tracer and Vosian police officer replied before they broke halovision contact.

Aboard the *ZIXC,* Gorn had awakened, still disturbed by the "panic" he felt in the vocal tones coming from the artificial worlds.

"I must speak with Kalt," he said, trying to shake off his increasing sense of panic. He entered Kalt's cabin and paused just inside the door, as Plas was there also.

"Captain," Gorn said, bowing slightly from his waist in honor of Kalt's status. "Captain, I am concerned that there is still unusual anguish coming from the artificial worlds."

I must tell her that I am certain that the one of the languages from one of the moons is the same as that from my space probe, he thought. *But how? Plas could ridicule me in her eyes.*

"Kalt, my dearest, closest friend—I know that you do not believe in the existence of cognitive beings outside the Geahan solar system. Still, I feel these being's unusual anguish," he said, masking his true feelings from Plas and Kalt.

"Unusual anguish. What is that supposed to mean? We don't know if there are any creatures inhabiting those moons that are capable of feeling. What kind of life form would live inside a moon when there is so much sunlight near? They must be extremely primitive. They have not acknowledged our search probe or our request for help," Kalt replied, willing her aura green.

"I want answers, instead. Both Plas, my first officer and you, the ship's doctor are creating more confusion, more doubts. I… we have to find a way out of this solar system and soon. The people of Geaha desperately need our serum."

The two officers who stood in front of her said nothing. Kalt turned pale purple around the edges, and continued.

"Plas, you are usually a very capable and supportive first officer. But you have been nothing but difficult. I know that you are terrified that you will catch the plague. We all are."

"The plague? But, Kalt, no one has caught it in space," Gorn said reassuringly.

"Plas knows that also. Still he and many others are frightened. Frightened beings make stupid mistakes."

"It... it was but a momentary lapse, Captain," Plas replied, sharp yellows mixing with his green.

"I have to make sure that you have regained your regular analytical behavior so that you can help me return home safely." Kalt fingered the only key to the locker where the serum was kept.

I must guard myself against a mutiny, she thought. *If Plas is desperate, then the crew, if not already desperate, will soon be. Now, Gorn is speaking nonsense. Perhaps the plague takes a different form in space, perhaps we are already infected.*

What if I am the only one not infected? Or worse, what if the plague has affected our minds? What if we are home, but cannot recognize it? I read somewhere that the plague has caused hallucinations. Perhaps I'm just imagining that I see three artificial moons and a large cloudy planet! Maybe I'm in a hospital on Geaha? Why hadn't anyone responded to the probe or to the Sixth Sheep? Kalt continued her silent reflections and double-checked the probes' messages that contained both the ancient and modern distress patterns. *Anyone in this star cluster should know my ship was in trouble!*

These thoughts and many others continued to crowd her mind as she floated in front of the ship's viewer and stared at the visible space stations, silhouetted against the cloudy planet. Kalt silently prayed to Goth, the highest Geahan god, the god of sailors, pioneers, and physicians..

"Please, if there are creatures capable of helping us. Help them to understand us," she intoned.

She made a mental note to sprinkle *vili*, or fine sand, on the sacred snow on Mount Ooua, in 'thanks', once she returned home. She dismissed both Plas and Gorn.

"But Kalt, I came..." Gorn began.

"I do not want to hear why you entered my cabin. I need time. I need to think. There is only one distress probe left. I have to choose the correct time to launch. Go..."

The tracers, eager to tell the others of their latest discovery or theory, began speaking over each other. Everyone stopped talking to listen to Olsen, whose voice dominated the conversation.

"I repeat. There must be someone or something out there. Someone who is trying to communicate with the Third Levelers." He stopped for a breath, the others waited as he continued.

"The Third Levelers have been throwing the bones and gathering for the Austr. No one can remember the exact date of the last Austr," Olsen said in a calm voice. He leaned back unsteadily on an Outpost chair, pushing the front legs a foot off the ground. He continued to fiddle with a toothpick, which he kept taking in and out of his mouth as he spoke. He frowned and looked around at his friends then paused as he waited for some else to speak.

I wander what Olsen'll do next, run his hands through his hair or rub his scar. Both are extremely annoying habits, Jamaica thought, as she waited for Olsen to continue.

He ran his fingers through his hair and cleared his throat, as if to speak, but he said nothing.

I must be careful about what I say. I am speaking over an open channel. Who knows who or what may be listening, he thought, again running his fingers through his hair.

In fact, two scouts from the *Clea* were listening to every word. McPeak's office communications had been "bugged" since the second series of *Clea* deaths.

"What's an Austr?" Jamaica asked when it became apparent that Olsen was finished for the moment. She moved closer to Olsen's halogram, which turned toward her.

Olsen righted the chair on its four legs and said, "The Austr is a tribal song to the Other Worlders. It is like a prayer of understanding. The Third Levelers consider all non-Vose as

Other Worlders. The Austr language is very, very old and has not been translated to good effect into any other language or any Vosian dialect. Each word, gesture or emphasis has a different meaning. Much depends on who begins the Austr, The time of day, sex of the originator and reason for song, etc."

"Great. We're in the middle of a mass killing and I have one of my best people dabbling in the occult. Third Levelers, for God's sake. What are you doing near them?" McPeak shouted. He paced as much as he could in his crowded office and pointed a steady finger in Jamaica's direction.

"And you. You think color is killing people and parrots are telepathic. What next?"

"What's this about a parrot? Is it No Pi L? What's happened to him?" Neils asked.

"Nothing's happened to it. It's gone crazy, like everyone else on this station. Talking to itself and having Jamaica here believe it's hearing someone outside the station. Nonsense! There's nothing out there."

Turning quickly for a man his size, as if defying anyone to contradict him, McPeak looked around at the three holograms, then to Jamaica.

Not known for her tact, McDonald, said, "I've been hearing things. I mentioned it to Neils. It's like... well... like someone's whispering in my ear, but there's no one around. I've been feeling it for two days. It's not steady. It comes and goes. It's very faint. Are you accusing us of making things up?"

McDonald shouted this in anger over Jamaica.

"I've had a difficult time getting to the *Clea* Outpost. I need support and answers from my colleagues. I don't need your 'attack'."

She continued over the others who were again speaking at once, each trying to explain why their "crazy" theory made sense. McPeak eased into his chair, as if seeking comfort and solace from its embrace. He listened to his troops, only to have the chair squeak, as if siding with the tracers. Sighing, he leaned back to listen.

"We all can't be hearing or imaging things. Something

must be trying to communicate. Perhaps it doesn't use words as we know them," Neils replied in a calm manner.

"No—it, or they, must understand and speak International English… or No Pi L wouldn't be repeating 'help us. We're caught'," Jamaica said.

"I thought you said the parrot was speaking nonsense," McPeak interjected in a firm voice in an attempt to regain control of his meeting.

"He was. Sometimes. But at other times, we heard him say quite clearly, 'help us.' In fact, Hannah asked that the two floors on either side of hers be searched—just in case someone was ill or hurt, who either did not have a sensing device or had one that was broken." Turning to Neils' halogram, Jamaica continued.

"I was at your home for dinner yesterday… I think it was yesterday. I've lost track of time. Anyway, after dinner, No Pi L began calling out, 'Help us' and 'We're caught.' He was very agitated. Carl Starr, from the *Galileo* zoo, was there as well. He and Hannah calmed No Pi L. It was so real. It was like he was trying to let us know that someone was in danger."

"That's the sense I'm getting," McDonald added.

"It's not anything I can define. I thought it might be the thought patterns of the Tapias. I don't know. I can't put my finger on the source," Jamaica said, shaking her head.

"I tell ya, McPeak, the Third Levelers are getting pretty stirred up. Something's provoked them. The whole planet's aware that something's going on."

Mariah entered the Outpost room in the middle of Olsen's sentence, only hearing the end of it.

"Something is going on," she said. "Entire families are packing to move back to Vos. There's an uneasiness on the *Bole*. It goes beyond the deaths of the traders. It's… it's sort of like a collective…" Searching for words, she continued.

"I don't know… sort of like people are being summoned or something."

"Summoned? Where are they going? Who will staff the *Bole* if the Vosian technicians leave?" McPeak asked as he turned to Mariah, but spoke to himself. When he turned in his chair the squeaks drowned out his next words. The tracers saw his lips move but could not hear what he was saying.

McPeak attempted to absorb the information he'd heard and said under his breath. "Parrots, crystallized Vose, burned people, Tapias turned to dust, Third Levelers, and something to do with color. It's all very confusing."

He rubbed his chin and thought again. *I need a shave.*

"This makes some sense," he exclaimed.

"There's some order here. We just don't know how to identify it. We have to continue looking. Olsen, Fitzsimmons— dig in and interview all your contacts. Retrace your steps, re-interview. Find out about these... these Third Levelers."

His face flushed to a dangerous color, McPeak paused for breath and loosened the neck of his shirt. Jamaica got up and handed him a glass of water.

"I just need to take these horse pills." He joked, shaking out two large green "*sman*" dosages, from his top drawer, and dissolved them into the water.

"Neils, McDonald, I've heard rumors about a Tapia flagship near Cassista arming itself against us. Do you know anything about it?" he inquired after a short coughing spell.

"How did they hear about the ship?" 0-6-93 asked, relaying the information with alacrity to 0-24-3 via secret code. The general, still on the *Clea* was trying to form an objective view about how his men died.

"He didn't want to believe us when we told him there is a conspiracy involving the Vose and the off-worlders of Earth. Maybe this will convince him."

"What do the Vose or Earthers have to gain by getting rid of us? We're better warriors than either race. The interplanetary treaty is still being honored. No, whatever or whoever was killing the people on the *Clea* is coming from somewhere else. Perhaps the Erns, the *Thane* tamers, have been making noises lately," General 0-24-3 said to the messenger, after reading the coded message from 0-6-93.

"No, it isn't the *Thane* tamers, it has to be someone who

wants to bring war to this part of the galaxy. And they know about our secret weapon, the Zyzzy Va," 0-24-3 said as he gave the newest message to Captain 00-4-69 as he entered the security pod.

"Yet the Earthers are not sending a ship here. Interesting. We'll continue to monitor their meeting," 00-4-69 replied as he tore the message into tiny bits and swallowed them.

"I don't know much. But there is a buildup of military ships on the far side of Cassista. The Tapias are meeting with the Maposian Divas," McDonald said to the group.

Another coded message flashed to General 0-24-3.

"The Tapias. What do they want with Divas?" McPeak asked.

"I guess they're meeting to negotiate for additional military support. The Divas enjoy the game. They would gain a lot of knowledge from a battle among the Tapias, Earth and Vos. But I don't think they will allow the war to begin. Too many unanswered questions. The Divas like to take sides when they know all the percentages, then they bid individually. No, they won't get involved until someone finds out who's killed the people on the space stations," Jamaica said, She stacked information discs on her desk while McPeak gave directions to the others.

"I agree. I don't think the Divas will get involved," he replied.

"Sir, I've been hearing about the buildup. Even if it is true, the fastest Tapia fleet ship would take a week to reach Vos. I've met, briefly, with General 00-4-69. He's a fair-minded, level-headed guy. He'd check out everything before going forward. He wouldn't allow an attack. We have to find out what's really going on," Neils said, as soon as there was a break in the conversation.

General 0-24-3 read the second coded message in his quarters on the *Clea*.

"Good. It is good to know that Earthers can be reasonable. 00-7-09, come in, prepare to transport to the *Cassius*. This message must reach Tusquets immediately."

"General." 00-7-09 bowed and walked quickly out of the General's room, went to the *Clea's* transporter and headed toward the *Cassius*.

Chapter 12

After he entered Voig's cabin, his first mate, Sese, waited for him to look up.

"Sese, I have been reading for the past four hours. I am certain that I know where the *ZIXC* is."

"Sire?" Sese asked, glowing purple, recovering at once and turning deep green.

"She has to be to the east, near the Ibso wormhole. The scrolls, the very, very, old ones from the Tone dynasty mentioned the opening to the other star cluster of a blanket of stars and a million planets, the star cluster where the Ayle clan traveled after their departure, a thousand, million years ago. The ancients believed that the path to the other galaxy was one way. But what if they were wrong? I believe that we can enter and return through the wormhole."

Radiating sharp blues, Voig continued to look at the scrolls.

"Sire, I mean no disrespect. But no one has entered and returned from the Isbo," Sese replied.

"I pray that they are wrong, because I intend to go in search of the *ZIXC* and return to Geaha." Still standing outside Voig's entrance, Sese waited for Voig to wave him in.

"Come in, come in. I cannot discuss our mission with you standing outside."

"We're getting dangerously close to the Hing wormhole, if the *ZIXC* entered it then they are doomed." Sese's purple alarm filled in the air. Holding up his left hand, Voig calmed Sese's vibrations.

"Don't worry," Voig said. "I think that there is a narrow

band of energy which could take the *Moor* into and out of the Hing wormhole in the identical path which the *ZIXC* traveled. The path should still have the *ZIXC's* thought codes embedded in the energy patterns."

Willing himself green, the excitement Voig felt nearly brought the heightened royal blue. He had felt royal blue only once in his life.

"I was going to send a test buoy," Voig continued, "into the wormhole, but was afraid that it may distort or destroy the path signals emitted by the *ZIXC*. We must take the *Moor* into The Hing. We have no alternative. I have read the old scrolls if the Ayle clan ventured into the Ibso wormhole we should be able to enter the Hing."

"Sire, no one knows for sure what happened to the Ayle clan," Sese murmured.

"You are correct. Since they never came back, legends grew that they had made it to the other side and would return one day. I believe the legend. If we are wrong, we will die dishonored. If we are right and bring the *ZIXC* and the serum home... we may save our planet. We are after all, sailors, explorers and physicians. We can do no less," Voig said. He moved toward the large, round window, which shook at the energy waves generated by the propinquity of the Hing wormhole.

"We should hurry. We need to send a message to Ncha and the Council," Voig said as he made a minor correction on the papyrus scroll, put it into the buoy, "...and sent it to Geaha."

"Sire, it would be quicker to open the thought channel to Ncha. He has called hourly since we approached the outer edges of Geahan space."

"He will attempt to talk us out of our destiny. He always tries for the reasonable thought, this is no time for that. Besides, the energy band, within the Hing, is softening. We need to move quickly," Voig replied and floated away from the buoy transporter. The buoy was sent and the *Moor* entered the Hing wormhole.

###

The *Moor* shook violently for a few moments, and then it appeared on the verge of ripping apart. Before Voig could begin corrective procedures, the ship became calm and settled into the pale lavender river of the *ZIXC's* thought tracks. The *Moor* passed through the Hing wormhole and entered the solar wind streams of the sun. It flew past Mbongo and was caught in the gravitational waves on the far side of Vos. Off to the left were three pale satellites.

"Those must be the artificial moons Kalt mentioned in her distress messages," Voig said with excitement to Sese. All members of the *Moor,* within viewer range, were staring at the large cloudy planet and the three smaller moons. They could not see the *ZIXC,* which was just below Vos' horizon.

Chapter 13

"Today, No Pi L, you're coming to work with me. I need to document the times that you begin your chant. Stop muttering, I know you know what I'm saying," Hannah said. She stroked the parrot and filled the deep water dish in his carrying case. He continued to speak softly to himself. She had not heard him utter the "help me" phrase this morning. After securing the internal windows in her office, Hannah let No Pi L out of his carrying case. He flew to the library case and cracked open sunflower seeds as she began her work.

Gathering the flamingo flashdiscs that she'd borrowed from Carl, Hannah walked over to his office.

"Hi, Hannah, how bout a cup of coffee?" he asked when she walked in.

"Okay—black, please. I'm returning this flashdisc. I haven't learned anything new."

"Neither have I. I know nothing more about how the flamingos died than before we began the investigation. I still think it's a virus."

"Yep, maybe it is."

"How's No Pi L doing?"

"He's fine. I brought him with me this morning. I'm trying to monitor exactly when he hears whatever it is he's hearing. Maybe time has something to do with it. I know I'm grasping at straws. This thing has me baffled. Well, thanks for the coffee. I've got to go."

"Bye. I'll let you know if anything turns up here," Carl replied and walked her to the door.

###

"Hannah in?" Jamaica asked the Jeeves 322 that staffed the Avian Laboratories' main reception area.

He replied while he scanned her ID badge.

"Dr. Daliz is in Section 3, Room 12, Ms. Wong. Follow the green stripes on the walls to the end of the third corridor, then follow the signs to Room 12."

"Thanks." She walked down the bright corridor.

"Hi Hannah, hi No Pi L," Jamaica said after opening the door and entering Hannah's office. She stroked No Pi L between his wings on his back and gave him a graham cracker.

"I brought these crackers for you to give No Pi L. I'm pleased to see him here."

"I don't usually bring him to the office. But he's good company at the lab. The other birds seem to like him around," Hannah replied as she looked up from her work.

"Sit down. Put those items on the floor."

"What are you working on?"

"Slides of the *veersi riia,* it's a rare speaking song bird from the polar regions of Mbongo. The birds are half the size of an adult hummingbird. You wouldn't know it to hear them. They have the loudest song of any Mbongoan creature. I love them. They are very rare and live a long time. But they haven't been transported successfully off Mbongo. I'm hoping to be the first to breed them off planet. Sit down, that blue chair is more comfortable than it looks."

"Thanks, you may think I'm crazy. McPeak does," Jamaica said and sat down among the halogram slides and posters that surrounded Hannah's desk.

"McPeak thinks everyone's crazy. Don't let him bother you. Why would you think I'd think you're crazy?"

"I came by to ask you if I could spend the day in your apartment."

"In my apartment, what for?"

"That's what I was going to ask. I wanted to spend the day

with No Pi L. I think he may be one of the keys to the station deaths."

"No Pi L? Why, because of his 'help me', nonsense? I thought you said it had something to do with color."

"I still think that it might. I just don't know how. None of the other tracers have a clue about what I'm talking about. It's just that when I printed information out on the info screen, lack of color stood out. But it's not getting me anywhere. So I thought if I could... um... if I could stay with you, here, maybe..." Jamaica answered. She looked over Hannah's immaculate, yet crammed office. Posters, holograms, and audioscopes of birds dominated three walls. The fourth wall contained a large, bright, hooked rug of several parrot species. A cabinet near the door contained small glass bird figurines. The entire office was calm and organized.

"If I could be here when he speaks again... maybe..."

"He—oh No Pi L? Of course, if you don't mind if I continue with my work."

"No, continue. I'm beginning to feel foolish as it is. It's just that something seems so familiar about No Pi L's speech. Whatever it is, it has eluded and haunts me."

"Like the melody of a song or words to a poem?" Hannah asked.

"Yes, just like that; something nagging in the back of my mind."

"I look forward to your company. You can make a pot of tea if you like. I have some Earl Grey in the cabinet." The two women worked in silence as various staff people came in and out of Hannah's office, some with documents for her to sign and others to pick things up. All looked with amazement at the small tracer working in the corner.

"Who's that in Hannah's office?" one lab technician asked another.

"Don't know, probably just a friend of Neils'. He's a tracer."

"Why would a tracer be sitting in Dr. Daliz' office?" asked a third.

"Why not? Maybe they're just friends."

"She's wearing her tracer uniform. Hardly the clothing to wear for a visit. Something's up."

"I agree," said the first technician. "Hannah's brought her parrot to the office."

"Did she tell you to call her Hannah?"

"She didn't tell me not to."

"We better get back to work. I don't know about you two, but I have tons of things to do besides standing here discussing Dr. Daliz' friends."

An hour passed from the time Gorn began his daily chant until No Pi L received it aboard the *Galileo*.

"Hannah, I think that I'm wasting my time," Jamaica said just as No Pi L began his cry.

"Help. Help us. We are caught. Help!"

Repeating the cry twice, he was suddenly very quiet. The parrot flew to the lab window and pecked at the leaded glass. Hannah rushed to the window and grabbed the bird. Looking through the clear, three-foot-thick glass, Jamaica saw nothing unusual in the clear night sky.

"My office walls lead directly to space. They are constantly monitored for leaks or breaches in the wall fabric by robot sentries. I don't hear the alarms. Everything's safe," Hannah said. She stroked the parrot, who turned his head toward the window.

"Do you think he's hearing someone out there?" Jamaica asked.

"It seems like he is. He has a habit of hopping on one leg three or four times whenever Neils speaks directly to him. This time, however, he hopped twice, stopped and hopped twice more."

"What is it? What do you hear? Are we the ones caught? Who's calling for help?" Jamaica asked, frustration creeping into her voice.

Gorn sensed that there were beings who understood the space language from his space probe and continued his chant. *Was the Sixth Sheep's chant reaching them? Did they understand? Was he attempting to reach life forms that were unable to receive his translations from Geahan? What if these beings couldn't understand the space language? What if the language was an ancient dialect which one no longer remembered,* he thought.

"I will keep sending Sixth Sheep messages through *RVIV*," Gorn said to himself. "I hope that there are Geahan ships that can hear me."

McDonald, on the *Bole,* began picking up shadowy *RVIV* words. Third Leveler elders who could interrupt Geahan, a dialect of their own Vosian language, read the distress message in the smoke of the bones, but did not know how to send an answer. No Pi L, like all Amazon parrots, a direct descendant of the AYLE Clan of Geaha, was able to translate the chant into his adoptive speech language. He didn't have the ability to let the Earthers know of his lineage.

Suba, The Moor's physician-empath, received Gorn's message. Suba raced to the helm and told Voig that the *ZIXC* was near.

"Hannah, I just remembered," Jamaica recalled. "I told you that I was familiar with No Pi L's earlier language. There's a Saari fable about the feathered peoples of AYLE, an ancient civilization that flourished a thousand or so years ago in the Saari forests.

The peoples and forest disappeared about 800 B.C. in Earth measurement. Many scientists on the Outer planets believed that dinosaurs, birds and *thanes* were all descendants from a common ancestor. Some Earth scientists discarded the dinosaur-bird connection in the late 1990s and have not adopted the Outer planet theory. What do you know about the AYLE clan?"

"AYLE clan? Uh... I haven't thought about that legend since I was a kid. I remember my grandmother reading me the AYLE stories when I was very small. What made you think of that Saari children's story now?"

"I don't know. There's something about No Pi L, his speech. It's... it's... really strange. Well, not strange. But the stories of the feathered Ayle peoples keep coming to my mind. What's an Amazon parrot to do with a children's myth?" Her voice trailed off.

Sitting at the desk, she began picking through the information flashdiscs on the deaths aboard the *Galileo, Bole* and *Clea.*

"Perhaps the answer's right in front of me, but I'm too tired to notice," Jamaica said as she shook her head and rubbed her eyes.

"I'm getting a headache. And what does any of this have to do with color or deaths or burns? You know, Hannah, I think I'm losing my mind. I know instinctively that there's a connection with all of this. I just wish I knew what it is and how to find it. What is the answer?"

Hannah didn't reply for a moment.

"I don't know. I'm going to pack up and take No Pi L home. Hand me the traveling cage, please."

No Pi L refused to enter the cage and instead flew to the window.

"Where? Where? We cannot find you," the parrot said in a clear voice. He turned his head to the night sky and hopped in place. Hannah and Jamaica stared at him, unmoving. He flew to the ceiling, near the corner vent, before they could react.

"Is he trying to escape?" Jamaica asked.

"No, he's clinging to the vent opening."

"Where are you? Give coordinate. Where are you? Give coordinate." He stopped to listen for a second, and then he flew down to his traveling cage and finished the graham cracker.

"Coordinates?" Jamaica and Hannah asked in unison, but

running in opposite directions—Hannah to check on No Pi L, Jamaica to call McPeak.

"McPeak, I think there are beings outside the space stations who communicate with color. Somehow Neils' parrot, No Pi L, can hear them. Perhaps they can speak, but we can't understand them," Jamaica reported to the rumpled frame of McPeak, which appeared before her at the secure halovision terminal in the Aviary laboratory's main conference room.

"Color? Jamaica I..."

She continued to speak over his attempted query.

"We speak, but communicate with music, sign language, gestures or smiles. I'm convinced that someone is out there, and they're trying to speak to us."

"And it does this by killing our people and the people on the other space stations? Pretty poor way to say, 'howdy,' if you ask me," McPeak said with a smile in his voice.

She continued as if he hadn't spoken.

"Perhaps they don't know that we're affected by whatever it is. They're probably wondering why we don't respond." She paused for breath and continued her speech like a child rehearsing a play. "Maybe they're trying many things. No one has died in a week. None of the alarms have sounded. McDonald's been hearing voices. Olsen's said the Third Levelers are throwing bones."

Raising a questioning eyebrow, McPeak emitted a loud sigh. *Magic and snake charmers, again, he thought.*

"McPeak, just because it's not scientific doesn't mean it doesn't exist," Jamaica said in response to the raised eyebrow and deep sigh. "McDonald is an empath or as near as we'll ever get. She gets feelings. That's why she's with the force."

"Yeah? What else ya got?" McPeak mumbled, listening with reluctance to Jamaica's account of the parrot, the AYLE clan and a recap of the last tracer meeting.

"It did sort of make sense. You have to admit that much."

"McDonald's gotten a little spooked lately. She's asked to return to the *Galileo*. She should be able to get here in five hours. You come to the office also. Perhaps the three of us..."

"And No Pi L?" Jamaica interrupted.

"What? I don't have time for any damn bird. I grant you it's a smart bird, but a bird nonetheless. No, keep it where it belongs, which is not in my office." McPeak's image faded as he broke the connection.

"You're wrong. No Pi L needs to be there," Jamaica said to the blank screen. The soldiers monitoring McPeak's office relayed the latest information to 00-4-69.

On Vos, Third Levelers began gathering in sacred *fyres* of six, seven or ten. The elders read the smoke.

"The smoke tells of two new voices. A weak voice, from the *Clea,* and a stronger one, which joins with the original smoke caller. Both of the strong voices are with *The Outside.*

McDonald heard voices. *I must be going mad. I have been in seclusion for over thirty-six hours. First there was the single, barely audible voice, which kept drifting in and out of range. Now this second voice,* she thought, turning toward the sound of the second voice. *I'll get myself killed. I've stopped in traffic, bumped into people. Thank God they thought me a Maposian Mystic.*

"Yesterday, it was yesterday, I think. I began talking to myself—like now," McDonald admitted. "I have to get off the *Clea.* McPeak's not returning my calls. Why should I have to beg him to let me return? Perhaps the disease that turns Tapias to dust drives Earthers mad. That's it! I've gone mad and McPeak does not want me around. Well, I won't stay here and die alone. What if I never called him? What if I just wanted to call? Where's a secure halovision? I'll call Neils, he'd be able to help me." McDonald unlocked the door of her compartment in the

Mystic sector of the *Clea*, and raced outside to look for Neils.

"Wait, Neils is with the Tapia assembly. He won't be back until after the solar eclipse. The voices are getting stronger and clearer. I can hear the words," She chanted as if reciting her prayers.

"Where are you? Give coordinates. Oh, no, the voices are coming from outside the *Clea*. They are becoming more desperate. Who are you? First there was only one, then two, now a chorus. Where are you?" she cried, her face vacant, her eyes mad. She, alone, aboard the *Clea*, heard them.

"McPeak, the Tapias are gathering to attack Vos during the solar eclipse," Neils' sub-space message read.

"They will attack from the sunny side of the *Clea*."

McPeak read the message and called for the tracers.

Chapter 14

The halovision toned as Neils was leaving the *Clea* outpost for his first *karasik* with 00-4-69, Commander of the *Clea* Interplanetary Defense Force.

"McPeak?"

"I received your message. Continue your meeting with 00-4-69. Your young partner here, has been trying to tell me that parrots and people who speak in color... oh never mind. McDonald's returning to the *Galileo*. She's got sun sickness. She's hearing voices."

"But she's an empath. She's always heard strange things. I could postpone the *karasik* mind challenge if you need me to return," Neils countered.

"No, I'm sorry I brought it up. I forgot for a moment. You're on your own. You have to convince a leery space station commander that an unknown, unseen, something is the cause of the deaths on all three space stations."

"I also have to slip in the idea that color's somehow important. That's not an easy task but I'm ready for the challenge."

The *karasik* would take place in a neutral place on the *Clea*. Both tracers and soldiers would be forbidden to enter the game. 00-4-69 paced the pale, blue floors of the *Clea's* main assembly chambers. By mutual agreement the chamber was the negotiation pod for the *karasik*. To his left, beyond the massive circular doors, 200 Tapias awaited his decision.

He had no idea what he would tell them.

Three feet away from 00-4-69, pacing parallel was Neils

Daliz. He also was uncertain on what he was to tell the tracer representative, in the information chamber to their right. 00-4-69 had known of Neils prior to this *karasik*, as the flashdiscs of Neils' negotiations with the Andromeda Cluster were a favorite viewing pastime of 00-4-69. The methodology developed during that *karasik* was a major step in military planning. 00-4-69 had the debates transferred via halovision to his home moon.

"I hoped to meet Neils Daliz in a more peaceful and relaxed time. I never dreamed that I would be chosen to represent Tapia in a negotiation sphere with... with my idol." 00-4-69 said, bowing to Neils.

I am to learn at the feet of a master, 00-4-69 thought.

00-4-69 played Neils' game. They talked, drank, swam, talked again, and viewed information screens of the deaths. Neils was good.

"I never thought that I would ever say this to an Earther. Not ever to the great Neils Daliz, but I find that I am liking you."

"I consider you also to be a very worthy opponent. I am honored to speak for the *Galileo* and tracers."

"You know that Neils Daliz' debating skills are the envy of the Tapia military elite. We are going to have a great game."

"00-4-69—your place in Tapia history is assured. Regardless what happens here," Neils replied.

"The *Clea* Tapias are convinced that Vos and Earth want the *Clea* for colonization. After all, it is the largest of the space stations in the galaxy," 00-4-69 said, and began the opening moves of *karasik*.

We desperately need both the Bole and the Galileo. I am sure that a new powerful weapon has destroyed their fellow Tapias. A weapon that I want. We would be invincible. The solar system would be ours, he thought, with the knowledge that Neils had overheard the other Tapias' conversations.

He also knew that Neils had found out about the ships near Cassista. But instead of asking about his information directly—an action considered extremely rude in Tapia culture—00-4-69 changed the subject and learned of Neils' discovery through indirect means.

"You are the first Earther with whom I have spent any time," 00-4-69 said. He closed his third ear to the loudness of Neils' voice.

"Your contrasts of logic and loudness are difficult with which to become comfortable. It is unusual to *karasik* with an Earther who purports to know more about my Tapia home than I."

"00-4-69, it is an honor to *karasik* with so noble a warrior. I, an Earther, can never know the pure logic of Tapia," Neils replied, neatly sidestepping a *karasik* Ur.

They had begun the *karasik* the previous evening. Neils had won round one, 00-4-69 rounds two and three. Neils, took four, five and six. Round seven was even.

00-4-69 looked over at Neils who looked up wearing an easy smile. 00-4-69 thought, *he reminds me of a* thane *I saw as a child on the grass lands of Er. The* thane *tracked, played with, then devoured a jutte. Well, he is not going to make me feel like the jutte. He seems to be tiring while waiting for the kill. We will see who is the jutte and who the* thane.

00-4-69 turned and hastened away from the closed doors, then leaned against an ornate *harza* wooden bench.

"Well, my friend," he said. "We have discussed deaths, the color pink, military might and have played games. I do not believe that a living organism turned my people to dust. It's a new weapon. One that may or may not use organic materials but a weapon nonetheless." 00-4-69 attempted to sound convincing when he hadn't even convinced himself. He waited for Neils' reply as they paced, each deep in personal thought.

Neils stopped pacing and blew on his hands. He sat near an exterior window, looking at the almost full "moon" of the *Galileo*. He smiled in 00-4-69's direction. *I wish I had my tracer coat. Why did I leave it in the hallway when I entered the negotiation pod? It's almost unbearably cold in this room. That's why 00-4-69's pacing. He needs to keep warm, to organize his thoughts as I. I'm sure we'd think better if we weren't so cold. I know that 00-4-69 asked that the room temperature reflect a summer day on Tapia. He's used to the cold. He thinks the cold will give him an advantage. But he's forgotten that he's been on the regulated heat controlled* Clea *for over eight years and had grown accustomed to the 29.4 Celsius.*

00-4-69 looked over at his friendly opponent and tried to digest the notion that Neils had discussed earlier, something or someone was attacking beings wearing a particular color. *These Earthers are more complicated than I have been told. Perhaps it is they who have the weapon,* he thought.

Following a long period of silence, Neils said at last, "I'm not convinced that something is absorbing color. I'm just restating the possibility. My partner, Jamaica Wong..."

"An Earth woman?" 00-4-69 interrupted. "You did not mention that a woman spoke this nonsense," 00-4-69 said with a satisfied smile that rivaled the *thane* smiles of Neils. "Ah, I have made a major *Moran* in the *karasik.*"

Instead of a direct response, Neils sipped his coffee and played with a small *hietpas* game while waiting for 00-4-69 to go on.

Aware that the female intellect was greatly valued by Earthers, 00-4-69 spoke, choosing his words carefully.

"Perhaps your partner can explain how the mere presence of color can cause death," 00-4-69 continued in his low voice. However, the contempt he felt for females, especially non-Tapia females, crept into his voice. The *karasik* shifted focus, 00-4-69 radiated confidence.

"The theory is that something is feeding off living things, which are composed of or surrounded by, or that ingest a substance of a particular hue. Plants, birds, *toyons*—anything with natural pink leaves, feathers or fur have died. You know this. I know this. Jamaica's theory has been discussed. We in *karasik* cannot discard any theory no matter how remote."

"A female," 00-4-69 replied softly and smiled to himself.

"Our own people have been killed or seriously injured. If it is a weapon, as you suggest, it doesn't belong to anyone on the space stations. This..." Neils searched for the correct words, and then he continued. "Came from outside the stations, outside Vos."

00-4-69 moved to a window and looked out at the night sky. The *Galileo* shined brightly at the top of his window. The *Bole* was still below the horizon. With his back to Neils and frowning, he peered at a ripple in the stars. *What,* he thought, *was that?* For a moment it looked as if someone had put their hand in a pail of water and disturbed the surface.

Rubbing his eyes, he looked again. Like all Tapias, 00-4-69 had excellent night vision. The ripple appeared again, resembling some of the jellyfish he'd seen in Earth's oceans. Again he frowned. *What was it?* He was so engrossed in looking at the ripple that he forgot for the moment that Neils was in the room, until Neils rose from the bench and walked behind him.

"It's a beautiful night," Neils said. *One I wish I were sharing with my wife instead of with a potential enemy,* he thought.

"Ah, yes. Beautiful. Nights like this remind me of home," 00-4-69 replied, suddenly startled into the present. He did not mention the ripple.

Neils gazed out the window in the direction of 00-4-69's unconscious stare and noticed that 00-4-69 appeared to have forgotten the discussion they'd been having regarding Jamaica's theory.

"Tea?"

"Yes, tea would be welcome," Neils replied as he scanned the sky. *There isn't anything out there. Yet, I'm certain that 00-4-69 saw something.* "What?" Neils said aloud, forgetting that the room absorbed his words to be replayed in debriefing.

His possible *Moran* momentarily forgotten, 00-4-69 had lost interest in the *karasik*. He waited for Neils to make the next move, with the fear that if he broke the *karasik* now, the Earthers would gain advantage. As anxious as 00-4-69 to cease the *karasik* for the night, Neils spoke first.

"Let's reconvene in the morning when we've had time to review the *haefer*," Neils suggested, to divert 00-4-69's attention.. Neither achieved *Moran*.

"*Haefer*," 00-4-69 replied with a smile, and relaxed for the first time since he'd seen the ripple. "Yes, yes... the *haefer*," he repeated absently.

I know that he's seen something out there in the darkness. Something that had disappeared before I reached the window or something only their night vision sight can detect. I must notify McPeak, Neils thought and strode out of the negotiation pod, 00-4-69 hot on his heels. They grabbed their topcoats and rushed in opposite directions. Round eight was a draw.

Chapter 15

Using the *RVIV* Gorn said to Suba, "Do not send a signal probe. The beings on these artificial moons are very delicate and extremely primitive. The way in which our probes absorb energy appears to be harmful to them. We have tried the Sixth Sheep but to no avail. They cannot understand us. I have mastered one of their primary languages, yet they do not respond. I know that there are sentient beings in the planet and moons, but they do not respond."

"I understand your concern. If you believe that I should not send a probe I will convey your message to Sese. He is getting ready to join you on the *ZIXC*."

"You must help me convince Kalt that my theory has merit. She has given me three days to make contact."

"What then?" Suba asked.

"Then she will send the final signal probe," Gorn replied in a low voice.

"The final probe?"

"Yes, the one stating that the expedition—that we have failed. I pray for her as she is getting despondent because we cannot return to Geaha with the serum. She has decided to send the crew to the innermost planet near this sun if all else fails."

"Oh, has she spoken with Voig?"

"I do not believe so. She is concerned about the crew. She knows that we will not interfere with the beings on the planet and moons near them. Perhaps there we could establish a Geahan colony. Everyone will be given the serum and in time our descendants could find a way to return home."

Transporting to the larger *ZIXC*, and bowing to Kalt, Voig said, "Perhaps, collectively, my dear Kalt we can reverse the wormhole effects and return home."

"Let's hope. Come with me to my cabin."

She led Gorn, Suba, Voig, Plas and Sese to the solitude of her cabin.

"When last we met, eighteen months ago, our greatest fear was the plague," Voig said.

"It is still uppermost in my thoughts. But our only hope of returning safely to Geaha may be to create a sling shot effect by using the sun's winds to blow the ships back to where, according to our calculations, the entrance to the wormhole should be. This will take the collective forces of both ships and intense winds to accomplish our tasks."

"I think, if we had an outside push, we could be blown into the wormhole," said Kalt, who was studying the triangulation of the *ZIXC,* the *Moor* and the sun.

"If only those beings out there," she pointed in the direction of the space stations, "were intelligent enough to help us."

"I believe that they may be able to help us. I don't think they know we're here, stranded and without power. Maybe we haven't asked in the correct way," Gorn interjected.

Suba nodded in agreement, saying, "I have been convinced that the beings in the planet and moon are cogitative. They are just unaware of or unable to communicate with us."

"Kalt, this must be the area where the AYLE clan began their journey into deep space," Voig said. He pulled out a scroll he had hidden in his sleeve.

"I have reviewed information in my library about our feathered ancestors. I am convinced our brother and sister Geahans are near here," Voig asserted, waving in the general area of the planet and moons, and continued.

"We must try to reach them. We must try the *Fourth Horizon* version of the Sixth Sheep," He said in a soft, almost reverent manner. The others gasped.

"The Fourth Horizon is the ultimate, highest Sixth Sheep.

It has not been performed, to my knowledge, during our lifetimes," Gorn said.

"Nor during the lifetimes of our parents or their parents' parents," Sese added.

"We are in desperate times. I've read the ancient scrolls. The Fourth Horizon is detailed in this text. We can do it." The others continued to mutter among themselves, but after a few minutes nodded in agreement.

"Maybe this is the only way those beings can hear us," Voig said.

"I will, with your permission, Kalt, outline the order and process for the Fourth Horizon. It will need to be performed aboard the *ZIXC* as the *Moor* is much too small for such a powerful incantation."

"My ship is at your disposal," she replied. "I will begin the initial preparation for the Fourth Horizon once you return to the *Moor*."

"I will gather my crew and inform them of the Fourth Horizon," Voig continued. "We should schedule it to take place in three days. It will take nearly that long for the clothing to be made and for the water to be blessed." "I will have the *vili* sand prepared. If we work around the sun, we can have the Mbongo, and the crystals purified," Kalt said.

"Don't forget the crew's own preparation," Gorn added.

###

During the next 68 hours the crew aboard the two vessels finalized their work for the Fourth Horizon. Gorn, in a purified state of readiness, ceased his chants toward the moons and prepared for the Fourth Horizon. McDonald's voices ceased. She slept for twenty-four hours, her mind free of dreams relaxed. No Pi L was quiet. His voices also quiet.

###

Prior to going home to rest, McPeak called Olsen and

Mariah on the *Bole.*

"Things are awfully quiet. The Third Levelers are hibernating. Something to do with the solar eclipse. Know anything about it, Olsen?"

"Not much sir. A solar eclipse is the most holy event in a Third Leveler's life. There hasn't been one that has affected the planet and all three satellites since they were built. I do remember hearing something about a great wind. I'm afraid I've lost most of it. It was very early in my indoctrination."

"Where's Mariah?" McPeak looked behind Olsen to the empty outpost office.

"She went to visit Serene, owner of Rick's Café. Seems that both the owner and the café have returned to normal."

"Patch me in to Mariah."

"Yes sir."

"Mariah my dear—have you found anything new?"

"No sir. It's really quiet. This place's usually busy. I guess I came by on one of Serene's quiet nights. I really have enjoyed the banter of the place. I think I'll miss this café more than most I've seen. I'm looking forward to my next case. Do you have anything more about the crystallized bodies?"

"No, nothing. I'm going home to get some rest. All this quiet is making me nervous. I better have my strength for whatever is going to happen."

"I think I'll do the same. I agree—it's too quiet."

McPeak finally went home to rest.

"Hi Mapuha, I brought you some flowers," Jamaica said as she sat on the side of the bed. Still wrapped in cy bandages, Mapuha reached out to stroke the sunflower petals one at a time.

"These remind me of Kansas," she said, her voice catching.

"Kansas?"

"I ain't never been there. Saw pictures on the halovision. Looks like a bright place, all them sunflowers."

"It is a beautiful state."

"Can ya stay a while?"

"Sure, things are very quiet. In fact, my boss went home to sleep. I think this is the first real sleep he's taken since... since what happened to you. What do you want to do?" Jamaica asked.

"You could read me a mystery. I love mysteries. Here's an ancient one by Terris McMahon Grimes, called *Somebody Else's Child*. I heard it is wonderful."

"Okay, *Somebody Else's Child* it is."

Resuming their *karasik*, Neils and 00-4-69 were even, both aware that the *haefer* did not support a *Moran*. General 0-24-3 finalized his last meeting with the Divas. *I am on my own*, he thought as he hurried to his battleship and crew of 200 of the fiercest and most dedicated soldiers from the *Clea* and Tapia. The Amazon zoo animals and birds in Vos, the *Bole*, the *Clea*, and the *Galileo*, slept.

After spending a rather pleasant afternoon with Mapuha, Jamaica changed for Hannah's eclipse party.

Returning to the *Galileo*, Neils anticipated the party. The *karasik*, in pause until after the eclipse, was a distant memory.

"What is so important that it could not wait until after the eclipse?" 00-4-69's High Commander's aide demanded.

"I tell you it is important that I see him immediately," 00-4-69 repeated.

"You cannot. He is aboard the *Myh*, 0-24-3's warship. He is not expected back here until after the eclipse." The aide dismissed 00-4-69 without looking up.

"Fine, I wish to see him as soon as he returns."

"I will let him know."

The High Commander is the only one that I trust with the news of... of what? Even I do not know how I am going to explain a ripple. Whatever I say it will sound as ridiculous as Neils' partner's theory on color. Still I must report the unusual sighting, 00-4-69 thought as he left the High Commander's chambers.

McPeak's halovision hummed.

"McPeak—new soldiers are arriving on the *Clea*. The *Myh* has left Cassista orbit."

The message stacked upon others received since he returned home.

Thirty-five people accepted Hannah and Neils' party invitation. Most needed little or no excuse to have fun, but some, like McDonald and McPeak, merely wanted a quiet afternoon with friends and co-workers.

"The eclipse should be at its zenith at 1 p.m. The sun, the *Clea*, Vos, the *Bole* and the *Galileo* will be in a direct line for 45 Earth minutes," Hannah said as guests arrived.

"Olsen, do you have plans for the eclipse?"

"No."

"Then join me at Rick's Café for a drink or two. You and I are the only ones who really know how to celebrate the eclipse," Mariah said with a deep laugh.

"I'll be there. Perhaps we'll learn something new and be able to finally complete these very baffling cases."

"You're right as always. Drunk people, regardless of where they are, sometimes tell more than they should. I'm counting on it," Mariah replied. "Besides, if you're like me. You're already restless for a new assignment. Preferably an assignment on one of the outer planets."

"Or in the Phoenix cluster. Interviewing relatives of crystallized people or trying to interrupt the triple meaning of Third Levelers is wearing thin. Nobody ever accused either of us of having any patience. See you at Rick's in an hour."

Aboard the *ZIXC* the Geahans prepared for the Fourth Horizon.

"Look, a *tyag*, the visible line up of planets and moons," Gorn and Suba said simultaneously, pointing their second fingers in the direction of the planet and its moons. Geahans rushed to the ship's windows and stared. A *tyag* was indeed taking place. The planet and its satellites were nearly in a direct line from a sun.

"It really exists," Suba said.

"Yes, it does. I know of no one who has ever witnessed a *tyag*. This solar system in which we find ourselves is indeed remarkable," Gorn said, his voice tinged in awe.

###

Raising their voices as one, the Geahans began the Fourth Horizon just as the *Clea* began to eclipse the sun. Two hundred fifty harsh, non-musical voices chanted into the crystal air of the *ZIXC's* prayer chamber to the beings in the planet and moons, then waited.

Reading to his men aboard the *Myh*, 0-24-3 waited.

Shaking their feathers after awakening, birds waited.

Dancing and circling above the smoke from the Third Level, butterflies waited.

Sitting in the corner of the living room No Pi L waited.

Guests at the Daliz' partied at full speed.

"Drink up, try some of my specialty, a Thai tea," Hannah said. She directed her Jeeves 322 to new arrivals.

Jamaica raised her cup of tea to begin a toast and nodded to McDonald and McPeak, who raised their wine glasses. McDonald dropped her glass and placed her hands over her ears, her eyes filled with tears, and she whispered.

"The voices. They've returned."

Over McDonald's whispers, No Pi L said, "We are trapped… Help us get home. Many are dying… Help us… We are trapped… We have learned that our search probes have harmed your species. We are a peaceful race… We are truly sorry… Our probes have been reprogrammed to use another energy source… We are directing it away from your planet and moons. Please help us… There are those among us who know your major language. Please help us… Do you understand us?"

No Pi L stopped chanting, nibbled on a cracker then flew to the large exterior window and settled near the lower ledge. He turned toward the beginning eclipse.

"What is that?"

"Do you see that?"

"What's in this tea? I could have sworn that..."

"Do you believe this?"

Asking questions of strangers, family members speaking to themselves, beings on the *Bole*, the *Galileo* and Vos saw faint bubble-like outlines of what looked like small ships. Behind the ships, stars rippled.

"They cannot be seen in the light. They must be transparent," Jamaica, the first to regain her voice, said. Staring either at No Pi L or McDonald, the others in the room were quiet.

Continuing to repeat, "The voices… It wasn't the Tapias," McDonald sat on the floor near the window close to No Pi L.

"We are Geahan… We come from the fourth planet of the dual suns of Geaha. We were caught in your sun's winds... We must return home… Many are dying… We have the serum."

No Pi L continued to relay the words from the Fourth Horizon chants, but he appeared unaffected by what he received.

"I don't understand this. No Pi L appears to be calmer than he has since we first arrival on the *Galileo*." Hannah said, inspecting her pet.

"What are Geahans?"

"Why are they speaking through your pet?"

"How can we help?"

McPeak stood near McDonald and handed her another glass of wine.

"You mean to tell me some aliens accidentally burned people on this station?" he asked.

"I ... I think so. The voices are the same that I've heard on the *Bole*," she replied. Her voice was steady, her eyes clear.

"McPeak, I think she should lie down for a while." Jamaica helped McDonald to her feet and walked with her toward the guest room.

Neils poured rum or vodka into half-full Thai tea cups, filled glasses of whiskey, straight, drained a wine glass himself, and said nothing.

The Third Levelers' elders read and reread the smoke, then reported to the gathering crowds.

"The ancestral cousins are trapped in the *Outside*. They need our help."

The smoke filtered through to the Second Level, to the First, to the surface and was carried on the wings of fireflies whose charcoal remains spelled out, "We hear, but cannot help. Try the moons."

Kalt took her place near the center end of the circle and continued to lead the Fourth Horizon. Only females had the ability to read the purified Mbongo of the Horizon. She sprinkled Mbongo over the Geahan home planet's image. She read the message from the Third Levelers, which appeared, then sank in a shower of emeralds.

"We have been heard."

"Kalt, I... listen... I hear a faint voice," an excited Gorn said.

"As do I," Suba replied over Gorn.

"They must be transparent," someone at the Daliz' party said.

"Do you sense a question?" Second Levelers on the *Bole* and in Rick's Café asked each other. Leaving their tables, work, bed or computer, each went to a nearby window. Scanning the pure black sky, they also saw the two small bubble-like objects rippled near the *Clea*.

"Are those ships the source of the question?"

"What does this mean? We are scientists, explorers and sailors. We have rid ourselves of the magic chants of the Third

Level."

"We explored the stars."

"We have no time for magic," they thought, collectively. They left what they were doing, gathered in groups of two, six, ten, thirty and walked to the main power housing for the *Bole*.

"All non-critical, non-life supporting power must be deflected to a point near the *Clea*," someone said.

"We must help," said another.

"We, The Third Levelers have the collective power, to change Vosian winds. We have never needed to change the weather. Today, we must will the winds to blow upward."

"Upwardly?" a young male asked.

"Yes, the winds must break through Vos' gravity to a point near the *Clea*," replied an Elder.

No Pi L had a captive audience hanging on each sentence.

"We must be pushed back to our entry point. We are trapped," he said.

Listening in growing silence, the Earthers looked to the parrot, then outside to the growing darkness, and again back at him. He hopped from one foot to the other, staying near the window and turning his head to catch every word being relayed from the Geahans.

Finally, Jamaica said, "I know this sounds crazy, but if there are intelligent beings trying to reach us and we haven't all gone mad... Then we need to help however we can. Those objects out there, which look to me like tiny soap bubbles, must be the ships of those beings, if they are ships. Soap bubbles float easily. At least, in Earth's air they do. They said that they're trapped. What if we blew them back to their space? What if we could create a wind storm?"

"What?"

"A storm?"

"With what?"

"How ya gonna do that?" several asked at once.

"You've all forgotten that we're on a space station. We can generate our own power. We can turn the turbos toward space, near the *Clea*. It's blocking the light. Maybe we can give them the push they need to get back home,' Jamaica continued.

"Craziest damn thing I've ever heard," McPeak said. Several similar statements from the learned assembly reinforced his statement.

"Push us back home. Yes... Help us..." No Pi L said, once again echoing the Fourth Horizon's message.

"I think that we can turn the non-critical power sources towards the ships," Teri Massa, the head of the *Galileo's* solar power planet, asserted. "We might be able to push them toward the sun. I don't think we here on the *Galileo* can do it alone. I'll contact N,gle on the *Bole* and Altz on Vos. Altz told me just before I arrived at the party, that the winds were really fierce today. He said that they started blowing upward."

"Upward?"

"Yes, maybe the Third Levelers have something to do with the wind's change. If he could harness the energy with that of the *Bole* and the *Galileo*, perhaps a triangulated approach might work." She walked to the private halovision in Neils' library.

"We can help," N,gle said to Teri's request.

"As can we," Altz replied. "The risk, if we are wrong is great. Yet, I cannot think of an alternative."

"Yes, we only have the word of these Geahans, relayed though Earth's parrot, that they are peaceful. If I have been misled... Have not beings in Vos and our stations died?" a cautious N,gle asked.

"It is dangerous. What if this push gave the Geahans enough power to destroy the planet and our stations? These creatures which we have not seen had enough mental power to stir up the Second Levelers," Altz added.

"Yours also? Earlier today, my men apprehended nearly two hundred Second Levelers intent on coming to the power station. They were not successful. They kept saying that they needed to help. I wonder if they had the same thoughts as we?" N'gle said.

Gee, it's only been 30 minutes it seems like a lifetime, Teri thought as she relayed commands to her staff at the *Galileo* plant. Her cold glass of tea rested near her hand by the power grid. *I don't remember bringing this with me.* She took a sip and stood waiting by the halovision with Altz and N,gle.

"We must be right," Teri said. "The Geahans must be a peaceful species that need our help returning home. I'm going to do everything in my power to help them. If there's trouble I'm ready. I brought Jamaica Wong, a tracer, with me as back-up."

"Hi."

"We have security here on Vos." Altz nodded in Jamaica's direction.

"I have a few trusted men with me also," N,gle replied, but didn't turn toward Jamaica.

"This is my first visit to the bowels of a station. I'm impressed." Jamaica looked around at the giant machines, computers, generators and furnaces, the "life blood" of the space station. Within minutes N'gle and Altz were busy relaying information to Teri for the triangular blast.

"Hurry, the eclipse is nearly over. The Geahan objects are fading from view," Jamaica yelled as the three operators readied their equipment.

Nearing the *Clea*, the *Myh* arrived near Vos from behind the *Clea* just as the eclipse ended.

"Things look calm. I am counting on the eclipse to lull the Bole, *Galileo* and Vosian personnel in to a relaxed state," 0-24-3 said to his second in command.

"I will find the source of the weapon that killed my men and claim it for Tapia."

"Yes, Sire. It will be a great victory."

"A great victory. I will have the High Command. Let 00-4-69 play mind games with Earthers, real Tapias take action!" *After today, my name will be synonymous with victory in this sector,* he thought, and smiled to himself.

"Shall we contact the *Clea?*"

"No. I have forbidden all external communication. They cannot reach us. And I do not wish to reach them until I am ready. There is nothing happening on the *Clea* that you need concern yourself with," 0-24-3 replied.

My attack will be a surprise. Troops loyal to me are awaiting my command on the Clea, he thought as he walked to his communications pod. Aboard his sister ships, young Tapia troops basked in the darkness between the *Myh* and Vos.

"The darkness is refreshing after so long in the sun," A young man said to his companion.

"Yes, it is wonderful. I have longed for the twilight of home. This darkness is most wonderful."

"Did you see old General 0-5-94 this morning? He was beaming. It must be the darkness."

"Yes, it must be the darkness. Today will be a glorious day for Tapia."

Emerging from behind the *Clea* just as the solar wind forces met in space, the *Myh*, ricocheted by the blast, bounced toward the *ZIXC* and the *Moor*. The Geahan ships bounced, then hurtled toward an opening in the Hing wormhole.

Recovering from the wind's force, the Geahan crews saw the familiar lavender river of their own thought trails.

"We made it," they shouted.

"Geaha is just a few days away," Sese said.

"Gorn, Suba, send a thank you to the beings. Let them know that we are on our way home. Quickly, your thoughts may not be able to leave this wormhole in a few minutes." Rushing from the Sixth Sheep chamber, Kalt took command of the *ZIXC* for its journey home.

"Thank you… We are on our way home," No Pi L said to those still at the party. Afraid that they would miss something, no one left before Jamaica and Teri returned.

"The voices have stopped. I know that I will not hear them again," McDonald said as she walked from the bedroom and entered the party.

Chapter 16

Arriving safe in Geaha, the *ZIXC* and the *Moor* crew rushed the serum into mass production. Within four days all of Geaha was inoculated. Deaths from the plague stopped.

"I declare a day of celebration," Ncha said. "It will take place in eight days, at *mosa,* during the setting of the dual suns. Meanwhile, Kalt, Voig I need to be debriefed. Come with me and the elders."

Kalt, Voig, Gorn, Suba, Plas and Sese followed them to the council hall.

"Ncha, thank you for meeting with me privately," Gorn said, glowing green with blue edges. "I must tell you what I have discovered regarding the languages of some of the beings on the other side. It is the same as on my childhood toy, the space craft which had landed in my yard."

"A spacecraft landed in your yard when you were a boy?"

"Yes, Sire. It was labeled with a battered pock marked golden disc and words. Once I heard the familiar language coming from one of the moons, I knew that the beings could help us return home."

Ncha listened patiently then replied.

"I do not wish to tell the majority of Geahans of your findings."

"Yes, Sire."

"They do not need to know of intelligent life beyond Geaha. The story is that a strange wind took the ships to the other side of a wormhole and returned them. Do you understand?"

"Yes, Sire."

Ncha glowed pale green as he rejoined the others.

"All of you will be honored before all of Gehea in the honored planetary ceremony of achievement, the *ndoa*,." he said. Green sparks arced in the air surrounding the others.

Kalt spoke first and recapped the events from the other side, raised her hand in salute to Ncha and spread her fingers to receive his praise.

"I believed the beings to be insignificant. They lived inside the planet and the artificial moons. Even though it would take intelligence to create the artificial moons, I didn't believe that those beings were capable. Yet, Gorn," turning to her friend, she continued, "He kept insisting that the beings were intelligent and that they didn't know that we were trapped."

The elders murmured among themselves. Glowing deep silver, Gorn, embarrassed yet proud, said nothing.

"Finally, during the Fourth Horizon... Voig's suggestion..." Kalt nodded to Voig who, embarrassed by the attention, also turned silver.

"The beings heard us and something happened. The winds, which had been silent since our arrival, blew towards us and pushed us into the wormhole. And here we are. Gorn and Sese heard the beings whisper to each other, 'we hope they make it'."

Her explanation concluded, Kalt floated to the nearest chair. The elders raised their hands in praise fingertip to fingertip, encircling the six. The entire group glowed pure green.

Following the awards ceremony, which took place during annual dual sun rise, the *mosa*, Geaha celebrated for four days. Five million Geahans learned of the Fourth Horizon and sent a message of thanks toward Vos and her satellites.

"Why was the Fourth Horizon being sent to the sky?" some asked.

"Do not ask me. I always thought the Fourth Horizon was a myth. I am happy to be part of the celebration," came the reply.

###

The *Myh,* battered for a moment from the blasts of wind from Vos and the space stations, its crew unconscious, its computer memory scrambled, came to rest with a pronounced list. Regaining consciousness, 0-24-3 looked around. Most of his crew was still out.

How did the Vose learn of my attack? The strongest wind came from there. How did they know, he thought, contacting Zyzzy-Va.

"0-24-3, Sire?"

"Return to Tapia. Somehow our plan was discovered. A surprise attack is out of the question. The planet's forces attacked me first with another new weapon, the wind. We are lost," he said into the empty air.

0-24-3's command was in disgrace. Limping back to the *Clea,* in defeat, the "weapons" were still not his. 00-4-69 met him at Port 12.

"0-24-3, your documents," 00-4-69 said. He extended his hand, awaiting the change of command.

"Sire, I accept my change of command."

It was months later, while on Tapia, that 0-24-3 learned his ship had been accidentally caught in the wind's triangulated forces, and that his attack plan had been unknown.

Returning to the *Clea* assembly to await the final round of *karasik,* 00-4-69 contemplated his next move. Neils arrived half an hour late and took his place.

"Greetings. We must continue for there are not any rules for stopping a *karasik* once it begins unless one of the debaters dies prior to round 18," 00-4-69 said.

"Yes, I know. But things have been happening on Vos, the *Bole* and the *Galileo.*" Neils explained the recent events.

"Humm... I must believe you although I felt nothing of the winds," 00-4-69 said.

His explanation is nearly identical to that of 0-24-3. And I did see something. Something that disappeared from this part of the galaxy.

Something that has a weapon we can use. 00-4-69 tucked the information in the back of his mind—*he would use it someday. Someday when he was High Commander of the Tapia Fleet.*

00-4-69 played badly. Neils won the *karasik.*

00-4-69 read a forced statement of acknowledgement.

"We acknowledge that no weapon existed which killed our people. A signal probe from an invisible species caused the accidental deaths of the soldiers aboard the *Clea.*"

Few outside Tapia knew that the forced acknowledgment was the beginning of a deep hatred the Tapias would develop for all Vose and anyone living on the *Bole* or the *Galileo.* The *Clea* became more militaristic and secretive. Personnel were rotated on a more frequent basis and the Tapias became more suspicious, even of each other.

Most knowledge of the Outside world was limited to three or four top Tapia generals. 00-4-69 was promoted to High Commander six months after the Geahan incident. "I will get even", he said to no on in particular, remembering with deep hatred the man who not only beat him at *karasik*, but also extracted the "accident" report he was forced to recite to his planet.

Epilogue

McDonald, comfortable in the knowledge that her voices were a fact, fully embraced her empathic abilities. She was reassigned to Mapu to study with the *Rista* and Divas and for a few months flourished in their complicated mind games.

"I want to go to the Phoenix Cluster," McDonald said. "I believe that I have honed my empath skills with the Divas. Mendes wants to go to Uranus. His undercover work in Ou has prepared him to take over my original assignment." She said goodbye to McPeak, who grunted his response.

"I know you'll miss me," she replied. "But mark my words, I be the Timossi's most successful female agent."

At the end of her ten years of service she moved to Maui, where she taught school and volunteered for special cases.

"I'm assigning Olsen and Mariah to the grasslands of Er. Some outlaws from Uranus' 23rd Ring have escaped to the grassland and are terrorizing the farm dwellers. They'll put order back on the plains in no time," McPeak wrote, in his final log as commander of the *Galileo*. He returned to Earth for his first check-up in over six years, after suffering a mild heart attack during the Geaha conflict.

"McPeak, you've done very well," the physician told him. "You should be very, very proud of the tracers under your command. You need to rest. I'm putting you on restrictive duty."

"Restrictive duty? You may as well plant me now."

"Come on, McPeak, think about it. You'll still be around young tracers. I'm asking you to teach first year cadets at the

University of Lisbon."

Lisbon. It is the leading university for entrance to the Timossi. And I love shaping new minds but I'll miss interplanetary travel, he thought, while his mouth said, "Lisbon. I'd love it."

Four years later, McPeak's body was found in the badlands of Cassista. With him were the bodies of two Tapias escapees from the military jail on Jian.

Neils and Hannah got caught up on life. Both had another four months on the *Galileo* after the Geaha conflict. No Pi L, who had grown quite fond of graham crackers, remained rather quiet. His dialogue returned to the pre-Geahan days. He flew about the Daliz' apartment, making a real pest of himself while he played with Hannah's new kitten, Jasper.

Jamaica revisited Mrs. Darrow, telling her. "The Geahans meant no harm. We believe that they are sincerely sorry for any harm, and especially any deaths their probe caused."

Those words, repeated words over and over again to the patients in the burn ward, gave a personal touch to things they already knew. The Geaha incident was on all the halovision news.

"It is comfortable to have you come and see us in person," Mark Kim and Shirley Van Cale said. They both progressed wonderfully and were released within six weeks of Jamaica's visit. Shirley sent Jamaica an invitation to her guest performance with the San Diego Symphony a year later. Jamaica never heard from the Kims.

Mapuha Smith was the patient whom Jamaica visited the most.

"Hi, how are you feeling?" Jamaica would ask as she placed sunflowers or yellow tulips in Mapuha's water pitcher.

"Fine. Doc says the bandages will come off tomorrow. I won't look like Tut's sister after that." Mapuha looked over to Jamaica. She sounded upbeat, a smile wrinkling the corner of the gauze.

"You'll be fine. No scars. You'll be back to..." Jamaica hesitated.

"Yeah. I'll be back to... but we'll still be friends. Won't we?"

"Of course. Besides, I'll be here on the *Galileo* for another four months. I'll see you often. Okay?"

"Okay."

Jamaica taught Mapuha the board game *GO*, and Mapuha taught Jamaica to laugh.

Perhaps that's why Jamaica spent so much time with her. She was so different, from the wrong side of the law, and she made Jamaica laugh. Mapuha still plied her trade among the Time Travelers, the scars were only on the inside. Some said that she played the meanest game of *GO* in the galaxy. She could be world champion. Except....

On earth for six months following their tour on the *Galileo*, life was returning to normal for the Dalizes. No Pi L and Jasper still played together.

"Don't you think it strange that a cat and bird played together like they were litter mates?" they asked guests, who watched the pets chase each other.

"No. Neils, do you think it odd?"

"Not at all. After all, they're both pets—even if one is brilliant and has been the toast of the galaxy. And the other has no idea he's a cat."

One foggy morning, ready for a day of play with Jasper, No Pi L flew to the large bay window of the Daliz' apartment and listened. The city was socked in. Pressed against the glass, No Pi L seemed to listen intently, then began to speak.

"We arrived, safely and in time. Thank you." He repeated the message over and over again, with the result that the Interplanetary Halovision news informed the residents of Vos, the *Bole* and the *Galileo* that they had been successful with their wind push.

Fireflies danced above the flames of the *fyres* of the Third Levelers. Word spread through the Amazon and permeated the fabric of the *Galileo*. The Tapias once again added the Geahans to their list of enemies.

Jamaica and Neils' returned to Earth four months after the Geahan conflict, their assignment to Er postponed for a month. They were to work the southern Oregon Coast Outpost during the winter vacation of the two tracers assigned there after taking their own two-week vacation.

"I can't believe it. Two weeks of relaxation before reassignment to Oregon, I've died and gone to heaven," Jamaica said to herself as she spent time getting her houseboat in order and visiting with her family.

Mrs. Wong stopped by the houseboat one day with fresh wild flowers and honey.

"Jamaica, have you seen Andrew?" she asked.

"Uh huh, twice since returning to Sacramento. Both times we were too busy to say much more than hi."

"Too busy?"

"Mother, he was going one way and I another on the steps of the County Administration Building, I said I'd call."

"Have you?"

"Mother, I will."

"Before you go to Oregon?"

"Before I go to Oregon."

A week passed. When Jamaica heard the low whine of a hovercraft approaching her pier, she stopped practicing a particularly difficult movement in Martinez Jones' last concerto. She arrived topside as Andrew approached, carrying a bouquet of wild flowers and a GO set.

"Hi."

"Hi, yourself," Jamaica replied. She kissed his cheek and took the flowers.

"Come aboard. Thanks for the flowers."

As he followed her below deck he looked around and spotted the crystal vase of old flowers her mother had brought earlier.

"I see you already have flowers."

"They're from Mother. She asked about you. Care for anything to drink? Tea? Pepsi? Orange juice?"

"Pepsi, lots of ice," He replied with a smile.

"I'm glad to see you."

"Me, too. How bout a game—like we used to?" Andrew asked smiling.

"Okay."

"I heard you playing. Your mom told me that you were going to be the guest soloist for the symphony again."

Lying across the back of an antique loom was the scarf he'd left behind nine months ago. Andrew noticed it, smiled, but didn't say anything. Jamaica perceived that he'd seen it but didn't say anything either.

"Yes, I'm going to play on opening night, in two months. Want to come as my guest? Tickets are really difficult to get, especially since Adams Kneeling is conducting," Jamaica replied. She began to set up the GO pieces for a game.

"I'd love to. Opening night. Umm... What day is it?"

"September 9th, Saturday."

"Okay...."

"Are you okay? You seem unusually quiet."

"I came over to tell you that I've accepted a position with the New America District Attorney's Office. I leave on September 15 for the New Colonies."

"Why Andrew I think that's fantastic. You've always wanted to travel to the moon. Gee, to be working there. I've heard the new District Attorney's really fantastic," Jamaica replied with a huge smile on her face.

"I haven't told my folks yet."

Jamaica looked over at him across the GO pieces. She paused, her hand hovered above a piece, waiting for him to continue.

"I haven't told your parents either."

"You told me before my parents?"

"Yes."

"You always talked things over with Dad before making

any move."

"I wanted to tell my best friend, first."

End

GLOSSARY

A

Aki: Jiangan liqueur, a favorite of JA Uru, the Timmosi Founder.

Alo: Saari fruit deep purple, taste like strawberries.

Audioscope: a 23rd Century compact Disc.

Austr: A Vosian prayer for understanding.

Ayle: An ancient clan. Common ancestor of Geaha, Third Level Vose and Some Amazon parrots.

C

Carpenter Barrier: A safety barrier established by the Interplanetary council to prevent dangerous or runaway ships from coming within transportation range.

Cassista: A moon of Jian.

Chancellor: Leader of the Timossi.

Coptic cross: From 15th Century Ethiopia, a commitment to Christianity, derived from ancient Egyptian used only in Coptic Church.

Cy: A poisonous Saari plant used in healing, dark purple in color.

D

Divas: A Maposian clan. Highly developed thought readers, excellent game players.

E

Earther: Mankind, indigenous intelligent dominant life-form on Earth.

Ens: A Tapia five player, per team, ball game much like indoor soccer.

Er: A moon of Jian.

F

Flashdisc: A 23rd century disc similar to a flashdrive but one quarter the size of a dime and manufactured with man-made metal.

Fourth Horizon: The ultimate level of the Sixth Sheep. Used in extremely rare circumstances for communication. Only a female can read the purified Mbongo and send the chant beyond the chapel.

Fyres: Vosian Third Level sacred circles. Elders who read the smoke of the bones can read Outside thought patterns.

G

Geaha: The fourth planet of the dual sun on the other side of the Hing wormhole.

Geahan: Indigenous humanoid beings from the planet Geaha; hairless, narrow eyes with hood to block out dual sun's rays; wide-eyed because of the planet's dimmer sun. Three fingers, opposing thumb, multicolored, iridescent, changes colors in light. No ears, small nose, teeth, and mouth, breathes and absorbs color, hears sounds through vibrations in their fingertips; invisible in sunlight; seen only as outlines in total darkness.

Geahan's interpretation of colors:

> Blue: normal
> Dark purple: danger/emergency
> Deep blue: worry
> Deep maroon: awe
> Deep pink: calm, soothing
> Deep red: vocal tone, male Bass
> Dull orange: sick/ infected
> Medium green: normal
> Pale green: calm/ sleep
> Pale grey: disoriented/ confused/ words blended
> Pale yellow: annoyance
> Yellow: normal

H

Haefer: Rules that determine if a *Moran* coup has been reached.

Halovision: 23rd Century interactive television/telephone.

Halogram: Image produced by person sending or receiving messages via halovision.

Haruko: Vosian plant whose fibers are used for space ships sails, like cotton or linen and once treated with water it has the strength of flexible concrete.

Harza: A hard Phuian wood dark green in color. Much like earth's mahogany. High polished it is used for tables, chairs and benches.

Hietpas: A Tapia child's game much like tic tac toe.

I

Ou: An inhabited moon of Jian "peopled" by blond haired, heliotrope colored, copper-based blooded beings. An ice planet famous for skiing.

J

Jeeves 321: Older model robot favored by historians and archaeologists. It is programmed for research.

Jeeves 322: Advanced robot which can be programmed to clean, cook, look after small children and pets. The favorite of single Earthers and young couples.

Juarez material: Material made of milkweed, dandelions, ragweed, Saari cy, Ul, and nently. A non-allergenic, and fireproof medicinal fabric.

Jutte: Small antelope-like Eron hoofed animals. Favorite food of the Thane.

K

Karasik: A twenty-round mind challenge. Winner determines negotiations for treaties. In the ancient past losers were sent to the inner rings of Uranus.

Karaski Ur: A trap.

M

Mbongo: a holy planet; also the water derived from the essence of departed priests used in rare Geahan ceremonies.

Moran: A major break of the Karasik advantage shifts... could affect next three rounds.

Mosa : The identical settings of the dual suns of Geaha.

Mych- a unit of Geahan time equal to a 20 day earth month.

N

Naresh- a planetoid.

Netsuke: Ornamental buttons or figure once used on earth to attach a purse or other article to a kimono sash. Fasteners on Tapia uniforms serve same purpose.

No Pi L: A sentient parrot, a direct descendant of the Ayla Clan. Extraordinary powers to hear and repeat thoughts. Has capacity to intercept a thought and find simple language to repeat it. Vocabulary of a 12-year-old Earther.

Noxa: a Gehan army ship.

P

Plea: A treaty, a solemn oath.

Poes: Geahan time.

R

Rista: Mystic followers of Yermo, a sub-culture on Mapu. Marked by a salamander stigmata capable of telepathy, a fanatic peacemaker.

RVIV: A Geahan empath thought process.

S

Saari: an Amazon fruit discovered in late 21st Century Earth.

Sixth Sheep: intense prayer involving all Geahans within sensing distance.

Sman: A green medicinal plant from the earth's Amazon basin. Used to treat hypertension.

T

Thane: Eron wild animals much like the earth tiger. It has yellow eyes and multicolored stripes. Large as a horse (Arabian).

Timossi: The Interplanetary police force much like the Texas Rangers of 19th Century Earth.

Toyon: A pink bear-like creature Native of Phu. Two are housed in the game reserve on the *Galileo*.

Tracer: A Timossi space detective, a police officer.

Tapia: Naresh's moon and its inhabitants. The military and scientific personnel assigned to the *Clea*. Humanoid, very large eyes; must wear reflective goggles on the *Clea* even on the dark side. Very pale, hairless except for blond queue much like ancient Chinese of Earth. Mate once every 30 earth years. Males produce 2 dark green eggs. Females fan eggs with webbed hands. Blue blood and cold-blooded. Women are 4th class citizens with no rights.

Tusquets: A political leader of the Tapia.

Tyag: An alignment of planets and moons in a direct line from a sun.

Tacqu: A mouth instrument much like the harmonica only sounding like a cello.

U

Urd: A fish-like creature on Vos whose dried bones are used for sacred fires and smoke readings.

V

Vili: White or black sand, pure fine as talcum, used as thanks when sprinkled in the air of OOua.

Y

Yona : A plant of the central Eron grasslands. Pink blossoms blooms twice an earth year. Pure juice used as narcotic by Thane tamers to give them strength. Diluted juices used for rum.

Yona Rum: Made from the hybrid Yona plant, a pink drink extremely potent and dangerous, 100 proof.

Z

Zi: Saari checkers.

Zyzzy Va: The Tapia secret weapon.

Acknowledgements

My profound and special thanks to Professor Anne Brice, Coordinator of Psittacine Research University of California, Davis, Carol Stulz, Sacramento City Zoo Education Division and Professor John Burns Astronomy Department, Mt. San Antonio College, Walnut, California for their help, advice and support.

To Charlotte Shoji for her insight into the lives of African Gray Parrots, which I used for my Amazon parrot in the novel.

And my great critique group, Ethel Mack Ballard, Jacqueline Turner Banks, Juanita Carr, Geri Spencer Hunter and Shakiri for all their support, feedback and encouragement.

To Cuz Rhett Neal for always remembering "the bad guys smoke tobacco"

Especially to my husband Richard for entertaining friends and family while I hid away in our office dreaming of new worlds.

Lily, Rosemary and the Jack of Hearts, used by permission of Ram's Horn Music (c) 1977.

order at www.pegasusbooks.net

ABOUT THE AUTHOR

Patricia (Pat) Canterbury, has written numerous novels for children, mid graders and adults, *The Geaha Incident* is her first Afro-Futuristic novel. Pat, her husband and pets live in Sacramento, her hometown. She can be reached at patmyst@aol.com or thru her website www.patmyst.com.